MURDER FOR JUSTICE

A.M. Holloway

Published By:

Your Book Company

eBook ISBN: 9781956648003
Paper ISBN: 9781956648010

Library of Congress Control Number: 2021918441

Printed in the United States of America.

Prologue

Blood. The color. The smell. There is nothing else like it. The anticipation of another crime scene causes Ellie's hands to tremble, making gripping the steering wheel difficult. As she parks her car, she readies herself for what she will see.

A group of men huddled behind an unmarked car, and when Ellie exited her vehicle, they separated. Then, finally, a police detective ambles over her way. "Hi, I'm Detective Larkin. You must be Ellie Masters."

"Yes, nice to meet you." Ellie shakes hands with the detective as she glances at him. Tall, well-built, close-cropped hair and gracious manners are a rare find these days. Some police officers are not so nice to be around with their arrogant personalities, but this one seems different.

Detective Larkin gives Ellie a once-over too and seems pleased. "Agent Watkins and I go way back, and he said you might give this scene a look. There's a lot of blood, and I'd appreciate your insight."

"Your call was perfect timing with my speaking engagements ending last night. Today is a travel day. So, we both lucked out. Are you ready to enter?" Ellie's patience is slim when a crime scene awaits.

With his outstretched arm, Detective Larkin shows Ellie the way to the front door. On the second step, the smell hit her, just like always. She turns and surveys the surroundings while settling her insides. The apartment complex sits to the east on the outskirts of Pittsburgh. This area of town could use a little renovating, with rundown buildings, unkempt lawns, people loitering in the parking lot, and other common areas.

Another police officer stands guard at the front door. Ellie and Detective Larkin sign the log and enter the apartment. A one-room apartment allows for a visual from the doorway. Ellie starts left and works right. Her eyes move as her brain catalogs was she sees. The victim is a male, maybe early twenties, African American, with tattoos and gang marks. He sits tied to a kitchen chair, gagged with his headscarf, and shot twice in the head with a small-caliber weapon. There are no visible shell casings on the floor.

Ellie proceeds toward the victim. His chest disturbs her. The killer not only shot the victim but carved a symbol into the left side of the dead guy's chest. Studying the picture, Ellie is unsure of its meaning. The carving is a horizontal straight line from the breastbone towards the rib section with an upturned curl at the end. Wonder why someone would carve a symbol? Was the victim dead before the carving?

Blood pools on the floor around the victim and in his lap. With so much blood loss, the carving must have occurred shortly after the shot. However, not only are there pools of blood, but there is also blood spatter on the floor, table, and kitchen walls. Ellie studies the spatter, beginning with the drops closest to the victim, and works her way out.

4

The South Precinct Police Officers watch Ellie work. Detective Larkin keeps the men quiet so Ellie can concentrate. He places his fingers on his lips as if he were speaking with children. The detective gets a snicker before the men stop talking.

Fifteen minutes later, Ellie approaches the group of officers. "Your perpetrator is left-handed. His gun and clothes would have blood blowback. These drops here in the family room appear that the shooter shook his hand off to rid himself of blood. The shooting occurred in the kitchen and was point-blank. There is a gap in the blood pattern showing the killer stood here when he shot the victim."

Ellie glances around the room to confirm the men were listening since she heard nothing. Detective Larkin stands with his mouth open. "You picked up all of that with a single glance. Watkin told me you are impressive."

A blush creeps up Ellie's neck as she replies, "I'm not sure impressive is the right word, but I have many hours of study in blood spatter. Watkins and I worked together in the past, but we haven't seen each other in a while."

"Well, he should be here any minute. Watkins couldn't miss an opportunity to visit with you. With his meeting in Philadelphia, this is a stopover for him."

"Watkins didn't share his travel plans with me when he inquired about this scene. My presentation had just ended when he called. With the information I offered, I'm hopeful you can capture this killer. He's wicked for sure."

As soon as Ellie mentioned the killer being wicked, Detective Larkin's face hardened, and his dark eyes grew darker. He glances back to the apartment, then back to Ellie. "Wicked? Are you saying the killer has killed before, or will he kill again?" Larkin whispers to Ellie.

"Probably both. I'm not sure what to make of the killing yet, but the carving is a strange twist. In my years in investigations, carving into another human carries a special meaning for the killer. The picture and its meaning will help find the killer." Ellie states while staring at Detective Larkin. She watches as his face relaxes and his eyes lighten.

"How many victims are we facing?"

"There is no guarantee this is a serial killer. I merely advised you on the possibility. You can probably catch this killer before he becomes a serial killer. However, this scene leans toward something more sinister. Check your records when you return to the office and see if any other crime scenes match this one. You may get lucky, and this is your only one with a chest carving."

"I'll check, Ellie. Thanks for your time. If I receive any other evidence, may I call you? My officers are canvassing the apartment complex now, talking with residents. If we're lucky, we can catch him before he strikes again." Detective Larkin faces the street when he hears another vehicle arrive. He smiles when he sees Agent Watkins.

Ellie witnesses the exchange between the men. Their friendship is genuine. Agent Watson greets the detective with a fist bump, then makes his way to Ellie. "How are you, Ellie? It's great to see you." He hugs Ellie in greeting.

"All good, Watson. I'm glad you found me in Pittsburgh before I left. This scene is messy. Detective Larkin has his hands full with this one."

Agent Watson looks at his detective friend. "What about this case is strange? Is there anything the FBI should know?"

Detective Larkin shrugs his shoulders. "As Ellie says, it's messy. Someone tied the victim to the kitchen chair, gagged him with his headscarf, and shot him with a small-caliber weapon point-blank in the head. Then, to top it off, the killer carves a symbol or picture into the victim's chest. Blood spatter is on the kitchen walls, table, floor and Ellie pointed out blood in the family room."

Watson looks at the apartment complex and then back at Larkin. "Can you get me inside to have a look at the scene?"

Chapter 1

Ellie tours the scene again with Watson and Larkin. As they discuss viable scenarios, she stares at the kitchen. The medical examiner removed the body a few minutes ago, so Watson missed the opportunity to view it, although blood tells its own story. Watson asks Ellie to walk through her vision of the crime.

The victim opens the door for the killer, and they walk into the kitchen. The killer subdues the victim somehow, then ties the victim to the chair and shoots him twice in the head. Blood sprayed back on the killer, and he shakes his left hand to remove the excess, pointing to the drops in the family room. The carving begins right after the gunshot. With the heart still pumping, blood pools. After Ellie concludes her story, she glances at the men.

Watson shakes his head. "I agree with Ellie. This scene is messy. Keep me in the loop if anything else transpires, especially related scenes."

"Sure will, Watson. Thanks again, Ellie, for your help. I'll call if I have more questions, and I'll email the file to you in case you want to take another look." Larkin shakes Watson's hand and strides off to the apartment.

Ellie stands next to her car, answering a text message. It's a reminder of her next speaking engagement in Maryland in two days. Watson asks, "can you make time for a bite to eat?"

"Always, I'll follow you. I need to drive back tonight and then drive to Maryland tomorrow for another conference in two days. Speaking engagements seem to be all that occupies my time these days."

The duo leaves the apartment complex. As Watson and Ellie turn toward the city, she notices how close the train station is to the victim's apartment. Is this the killer's mode of transportation? As she follows Watson, she thinks about how life brought them together. With expert witness status, Ellie doesn't investigate crimes anymore as part of a police department unit. Instead, she spends her time giving lectures at conferences or in trials and occasionally consulting with the FBI. While in Montana at a speaking engagement, Agent Watson introduced Ellie to Digger. They struck up a friendship, and she assisted with Digger's investigation. During the investigation, the killer stabbed Ellie because she favored her victims. However, Digger and Watson saved her life. Cold chills still run up her arms when she touches the scar.

Dinner is pleasant as two friends catch up on life. Agent Watson asks Ellie about Digger. Ellie admits to not seeing Digger lately, but they speak on the phone often. A ding sounds from Ellie's side of the table, and she glances at her phone, noticing a recent email. Shifting her eyes upward, Watson stares at her. "What's wrong?"

"Larkin sent the file already. He works fast if he can produce a file that quickly." Ellie drops her phone into her purse and finishes her meal. As she places her napkin on the table, her phone rings. "Larkin must be eager for me to look at the file." She plucks her cellphone out from the bottom of her handbag and blushes. "Digger is calling. I'll call him later."

"He'll want to hear about the investigation. You know he's been studying blood spatter since he met you. Please don't tell him I told you. He'll be mad at me." Watson says with a lopsided grin on his face.

Ellie's eyebrows raise as she studies Watson to see if he's telling the truth. "Yes, I'm speaking the truth. He'll prove it to you." Watson confirms.

With dinner over, the duo walks outside and says their goodbyes at the car. Ellie climbs into her vehicle and settles behind the wheel. When she's on the road heading for home, she dials Digger. There is joy in Digger's voice when he hears hers. The drive home is quick since they speak the entire trip. Ellie also piques Digger's interest in the carving case, so he makes it easy to discuss scenarios. Finally, she invites Digger to visit this weekend since her week ends after her Maryland conference. He jumps at the chance to visit.

Ellie's week closes with a Maryland lecture in a packed auditorium. More people showed than Ellie expected. Her speech topic is Blood Spatter, and pictures of the latest crime scene come to her mind. Detective Larkin wants a return call, and Ellie hasn't done it yet. Many people stay behind at the lecture hall for a chance to meet Ellie. They produce paper and pen for her autograph, and she obliges until she satisfies the last one.

When Ellie leaves the building, she notices the gorgeous sunset, with pinks and orange molded together. It is chilly for late spring but still pretty, with roses in bloom. Just as Ellie reaches for her door handle, her phone rings. While searching her purse for her phone, she notices a pair of shoes in her line of vision. Startled, Ellie tries to step back, but her car prevents her. She looks up into an unknown man's face. He isn't smiling, as he carries no expression. A piece of paper crinkles in the breeze, and Ellie glances down to see it. The man holds a single piece of paper and a black pen.

"Hi, can I help you?" Ellie asks in a shaky voice as her voicemail sounds for a message.

He doesn't give a response. Instead, he pushes the paper and pen toward her.

Assuming he wants an autograph, Ellie takes it from him and scribbles her name to the paper. She hands it back to him, and he turns and walks off, never uttering a word.

Ellie hurries to enter the confines of her car. Once inside, she locks the doors and glances around the lot. No one witnessed the exchange with the strange man. She shakes her head, trying to forget it. Then she remembered the voicemail. As she listened to it, she chuckled because it was another spam call. Her drive home was uneventful, which helped her uneasiness.

The following day, Ellie prepares for Digger's visit. She races around her apartment, making sure everything is in its proper place. Digger has never visited her before, although she has been to his place several times on her way back home from a speaking engagement. She wants everything perfect.

While waiting for Digger's arrival, Ellie dials Detective Larkin. He answers on the first ring to Ellie's apologies for not calling sooner. Detective Larkin admits they have no additional evidence on the murder east of Pittsburgh. However, the medical examiner also stated the carver was left-handed. Ellie advises she received his file and will study the pictures again. The medical examiner confirmed the victim was deceased at the time of the carving. With the confirmation, Ellie expresses her relief. Detective Larkin asks Ellie to call if she discovers any fresh evidence, and they will continue working on it, too. After the call, Ellie stares at the phone, wondering the real reason for the phone call.

A soft knock on the front door alerts Ellie to Digger's arrival. She jumps up from the chair and places the case file on the counter on her way to the door. Taking a deep breath, she opens the door to an enormous bouquet. Digger grins so big as he shoves the flowers into Ellie's hands and picks her up and twirls her around. He places the softest kiss on her lips, and the gesture renders her speechless.

"It's so good to see you. Too much time has passed since I saw you last." Digger said, gushing at Ellie.

Ellie steps away from the door, looking at the bouquet. "Oh, Digger. These are gorgeous flowers, and the fragrance is delightful. My vase collection isn't extensive, as I don't have a vase large enough for the bouquet. However, I'll split them into two arrangements. We can enjoy them from the kitchen counter and the dining table." Ellie walks into the kitchen with Digger on her heels. "I made reservations for dinner, assuming you are hungry."

"You know me. I can always eat. What's this?" Digger picks up the file from Detective Larkin. He thumbs through the pictures and moans every so often. Then he reads the scene's description. "The killer carved a symbol or picture into the victim. That's strange. We discussed this murder yesterday on your drive. I understand why you labeled it messy."

"I wish you could've seen it in person. Blood spatter is my specialty, but this took it to an extra level. Once I settled my stomach, I found where the shooter stood, and they were looking for a left-handed shooter. Also, the medical examiner agreed the carver was left-handed. We assume the shooter and the carver are the same person."

Digger notices the address of the crime scene. "The location is questionable. How did you end up there?" He asks with his eyebrows raised.

Unsure of Digger's tone, Ellie explains the relationship between Watson and Detective Larkin. She continued with her lecture being close to the scene, so she agreed to meet the two men and view the scene in person. Detective Larkin and the other officers were taken aback by the spatter. Ellie reaches for the crime scene photos and lays them out on the kitchen table in a sequence of how she saw the scene: from the doorway and left to right.

Regardless of tenure, this scene will stay with a person forever, and Digger recognizes it. "The killer is not done. This is the work of a serial killer. Are there any other murders in the area with the same attributes?"

"Detective Larkin is looking into the possibility. You and I will visit this weekend. If you're still hungry after the photos, we need to get a move on before someone takes our table."

Digger takes Ellie's hand, and they walk out the door. As Digger leans in to turn out the light, he takes one last glance at the photos, and a shiver runs up his spine.

Chapter 2

Ellie and Digger enjoy a late breakfast, sightseeing, shopping, and a stop by Ellie's favorite coffee house. Their relationship is progressing into something more permanent, but one must move for the other. There have been no discussions about living arrangements yet, but Ellie expects it. Her phone rings while sitting on the patio of the coffeehouse. She contemplates whether to answer, but she gives in, then regrets the move.

"Agent Watson, how are you? I'm sitting at my favorite coffee house with Digger, enjoying my special drink. You what? The scene is an hour or more away from here. How did you hear about it? Hold on. I'll put you on speaker. No one is around, so we can speak freely."

Digger speaks, "Hi, Watson. What are you dragging Ellie into this time?"

"Hello to you too, Digger. If memory serves me, she stayed back in Montana to help you."

"Okay, guys. Enough with the banter. Tell us what you have, Watson." Ellie states.

"Another detective unit contacted me through my statewide alert about Larkin's last murder. They also have a similar one. The victim has been dead for about thirty-six hours, the best they can tell from speaking with his co-worker. Someone bound him to a chair, gagged, and shot him in the head. Can you make the trip? I offered your services. Digger, you can tag along too."

"Watson, you have awful timing. She need not go alone as the other scene wasn't someplace for a lady to venture alone. I can imagine this place is the same."

"Digger, you're correct, and murder doesn't have a timetable. I'll text the address to Ellie's phone. Nice to chat with you both. Call me when you get there."

When the call ends, Digger and Ellie exchange glances. That call breaks their spirits. "Sorry, Digger, for the change in our plans. Watson seems to interrupt the best weekend, but the sooner we get to the scene, the sooner we get back."

The pair climbs into the car for the trip north of Pittsburgh. As soon as they enter the interstate, Ellie receives a text with the address for the scene. Digger searches the internet for any information on this area of Pittsburgh. "Just as I suspected, this area is unstable. If this is the same killer, he is targeting younger males. Is this the second murder with the same characteristics?"

"I know of only two. No one has mentioned to me that there are more. Agent Watson didn't share with me. He sent out an alert to other agencies in Pennsylvania."

Ellie turns when the cell phone robotic voice instructs. She glances at Digger, grateful for his presence. This area is worse than the last one. People loiter on every street corner and in doorways. Iron bars cover the building windows, and that means one thing, crime happens here.

On the next right, flashing lights and emergency vehicles greet them. Ellie steers the car into a spot on the side of the road since police tape closes the lot. Ellie and Digger walk up to the police officer guarding the scene and show their IDs. They sign the logbook, and the officer lifts the tape, granting them entrance. The apartment complex faces a road with parking in the front and scrub bushes and trees bordering three sides. Officers file out of the apartment, and Ellie introduces herself to the first one. He nods his head without a word and points his finger up the steps.

Digger guides Ellie up the steps toward another group of people. A man facing away from Ellie turns toward her when he hears someone approaching. Ellie gasps when she recognizes the man. "Ellie Masters. I didn't know you were coming, but I'm glad you did. We can use your skills. How have you been? Who is your friend?"

Ellie stammers as she regains her strength to stand and brings her mind into focus. "This is Chet Collins. He is a fellow forensic scientist. Chet, this is Detective Marshall Beck."

"Nice to meet you, Detective Beck. Can you show us around? We need to get back on the road once we view the scene." Digger explains curtly. He's uncertain what to make of Ellie's reaction to seeing Marshall Beck. Did those two have a past? If so, what happened?

Marshall takes the lead and ushers the pair into the apartment. Ellie stops at the doorway and surveys the area. The metallic blood smell sends her stomach into flips. Once it settles, she moves left to right. They end in the kitchen area. The apartment has an open floor plan with the family room, kitchen, and dining area steps apart. Blood covers the kitchen from the floor to the cabinets, both above and below the counter. They removed the victim before Ellie's arrival. She asks pertinent questions about how the body was seated when they discovered him.

The crime scene guy describes the victim and proves his version with photos from his camera. The images confirm the time of estimated death. Ellie questions the victim's chest condition, and Marshall glances at Ellie with a quizzical expression. "What can you tell me about this murder?"

Ellie first looks at Digger and gets a nod before explaining the crime scene from the other day. She tells the story, beginning with her lecture, receiving a call from FBI Agent Watson, meeting with Detective Larkin, and now here. "There is one other thing about your killer. Your killer is left-handed. He stood right there when he fired the gun. If there is a carving on his chest, then I say this is the same killer as the others."

With a slight cough, the crime scene tech faces the group and flashes the picture of the latest chest carving. It is a horizontal straight line carved into the left side of the victim's belly. The carving sits to the side of the naval. Ellie sucks in a breath as Marshall swears. Marshall runs his hands through his hair and paces. "This victim is Asian and works in an eatery. A co-worker found him when he didn't show for work. Our medical examiner suspects someone killed the victim approximately thirty-six hours before the co-worker found him. I'll head back to the office and see what I can find on our victim."

"It's good to see you, Marshall. It's been a long time." Ellie says as she eases away from him. She wants to leave and head back home, but Marshall places his hand on Ellie's arm.

"It has been too long. I'm glad you came to the scene. Can I send you the file and keep in touch?" Marshall asks in a hopeful tone.

"Sure, Marshall." Ellie hands him a business card and turns and walks to the car. Marshall studies the way Digger guides Ellie through the crowd. What is their relationship?

Ellie turns, "Marshall, what tied the victim to the chair?"

"It appears to be his headscarf. I only glanced at it before the crime scene guys bagged it for evidence. I'll include the photos of the scene in the case file. Does it mean anything?"

"It might. Thanks, Marshall." Ellie turns toward Digger when he receives a call.

"Watson, we just finished with our scene, and now we are heading back to Ellie's. What? Are you kidding me? My gear is at home. Let me discuss it with Ellie. Hold the line, Watson."

Digger explains things to Ellie loud enough for Watson to hear. "Ellie, this guy is messing up our weekend. Now, he wants me to meet him at a scene close to your first scene, of all places. They found a pile of bones in a condemned house."

"Really? That is a coincidence if I've ever heard of one. We can be there in an hour."

"Watson, we're on our way. Send me the address." Digger sees Marshall walking toward the car.

"Everything okay?" Marshall inquires.

Ellie explains another crime scene east of Pittsburgh involving bones, and Digger specializes in bone recovery. Then Digger adds they discovered the bones in a crawl space when crew members checked out a home for demolition.

Marshall states, "I guess Larkin gets another one. Lucky for him." He waves his hand as he walks to his vehicle. With his book in hand, he makes notes about the scene and Ellie's observations. At the bottom of the page, he draws a heart around Ellie's name.

The trip out east is longer than expected because of traffic. Ellie and Digger discuss the crime scenes and their similarities. Digger ponders the notion of two killers using the same attributes to murder someone. He knows the probability is slim. Have there been more murders with chest carvings?

Agent Watson meets the duo at the driveway's edge. Both exit the car and stretch. Watson strolls over to the pair and shakes their hands. "Thanks for coming. It's time for a little background on this scene. The state purchased the houses in this neighborhood from their owner or condemned them if they couldn't locate the owners. Two remaining condemned homes are ready for demolition, but the workers discovered bones in the crawl space of one home. They're not animal bones. I'm describing multiple skeletons, some on top of the soil, and some buried."

"How long has the home been vacant, and who owns it?" Digger asks as he surveys the area.

"We're not sure. The county is investigating that for us. Detective Larkin will handle it." Watson looks at Ellie and says, "you met him earlier at the murder scene a few days ago."

"I remember. Digger and I noticed similarities between his murder case and the one from today. Detective Beck will send his case file to me for review."

"After you review them, will you let me know your thoughts?" Watson sounds like he is pleading for help with this. Is he preparing for a serial killer?

Digger walks to the front door, stops, then surveys his surroundings before entering. The subdivision is a typical older one. It boasts larger lots, with some homes being one, two, or three stories. This home is a ranch-style home with a two-car carport attached at the kitchen end. As Digger walks in, men speak in hushed tones in the kitchen area. One guy stops Digger. "Hey, who are you?"

"I'm Chet Collins, here at the request of FBI Special Agent Watson."

"Oh, yeah, you're Digger. We've been waiting for you." The crime scene guy continues, rattling off a half dozen names and titles. The entire time, Digger stares. His mind goes blank when people try to introduce him to multiple people at once. He'll never remember them, so why try? The guy sees Digger's confused look and shows him off to the crawl space.

Watson and Ellie walk into the house together. The group introduces themselves again to Ellie, and she shuffles up behind Digger. "Are you ready to see it? If so, lead the way." All eight people walk down the steps into the yard. They walk left around the corner of the yard to a small door cut into the side of the house. Ellie glances at Digger and shakes her head. All these people can't go under there together, and she doesn't like crawl spaces or attics, so she bows out.

Digger glances at the men. "Which one of you found the bones?"

The talkative guy answers, "I did."

Pointing at the guy, "You lead the way." Digger leans over and opens the door. He plucks his penlight from his pants pocket and points under the house.

The leader gets down on all fours, then falls to his belly and shimmies into the tight space. As they get further from the doorway, Digger notices the downhill slope, allowing him to get on his knees without hitting his back. The area above his head is higher than when he began. "Is the space deep enough for a recovery investigation?"

"I'll let you decide. My expertise in crimes involves murder with bodies, not bone recovery. Two men on the demolition team discovered the bones. They were setting charges under the house because they scheduled demolition for Monday."

"Are the charges active now? I would hate for someone to think it's okay to hit the button." Digger asks with worry, edged into his voice.

"No, they're not charged. We removed the charges when we arrived at the scene because we didn't want an accident to occur while we were investigating it."

Digger lets out a breath when he hears the reply. Arriving at the site, Digger adjusts his face mask. Then he snaps photos with his cell phone and dictates a few crucial facts into his voice recorder. The crime scene guy slides out of the way and watches Digger's work. "I'm here visiting a friend when Watson calls for our help. Using a paintbrush is not how I usually operate. Any idea how many skeletons we are looking at here?"

"No. There are two visible skulls, but we found too many bones for just two people. We're assuming they buried more skulls. What tools do you need? I'll try to round them up for you."

"You can't find them at the local store. I'll use whatever we have. Is there a small shovel or spoon and a sifter? If you think they buried more, then I'll sift the dirt. The work is tedious but worth it."

"I'll be back in a second. Also, we have lights and body bags coming."

Digger replies with grunts, and he begins his process of brushing the soil with a paintbrush. As he looks around, the crawl space is cleaner than he expected. Someone dug this area out by hand over an extended period. Was its purpose a mass grave? How did these people get in here? Digger scans the floor of the house, searching for a way into the space. He crawls a little further and sees a strange piece of wood. It differs from the rest of the house.

Using this floor opening to transport the victims to the crawl space might open into a room. Digger dials Ellie's number. Once she answers, Digger explains his theory and asks her and Watson to enter the house. He'll knock on the odd wood piece until one of them locates the sound. If they can open it, he'll have more light and a more natural way to help with recovery.

Digger bangs on the floor above his head until Watson yells at him to stop. "A guy is bringing a crowbar to us so we can open it. Someone concealed the hole in the bedroom floor for a reason. Now, we know why. Crawl backward, Digger. We'll open it now."

Two minutes pass when the floor opens wide. Sunlight pours into the hole from the bedroom window. "Nice to see you two." Digger grins, looking up at Ellie and Watson.

"Ellie, this might take me an hour. Are you okay with waiting?" Digger inquires.

"Detective Beck sent me the case file from the earlier scene. I'll sit in the car and peruse it while you take care of things down there." Ellie answers as she turns and walks off towards the car.

After Ellie is out of earshot, Digger throws out a question. "Hey, Watson. What do you know about Detective Marshall Beck?"

"He's been around a long time. The FBI tried to hire him, but he refused the offer. He claims he wants to stay in the community. Why are you asking?"

"Detective Beck is the lead detective on the second murder scene. Ellie and Beck shared strange facial expressions when they saw each other. I wondered if they have a past."

"Well, Digger. Ask her yourself. I am not privy to every man she has dated."

Someone lowers a sifter and a small shovel into the crawl space through the floor opening, and it lands at Digger's feet. He glances up, but no one is visible. The crime scene guy seems impressed by the floor. Digger works for almost an hour when the two remaining skulls appear in the dirt. Brushing off the skulls, he inspects them. The cause of death is undetermined by visual inspection. The medical examiner graciously offered their services for the bones.

"Send down four body bags," Digger yells up through the hole. "I'll also need someone to help with packaging."

Four bags, and a person descends through the hole using a ladder. The hole and the ladder help speed the process. Crawling in and out of this space would be a time-waster. Digger unfolds the bags on the soil and places one skull into each bag. Digger sets the bones found closest to the skulls inside the corresponding bag. Then he puts the scattered bones in the bottom of a bag in a separate compartment.

The crime scene guy ushers Digger up the ladder first. Then they work in tandem, lifting the bags into the house. Someone from the yard yells, "Digger, the medical examiner's office is here. Can you speak with them?"

"Yes, I need to explain my recovery procedure." Digger walks to the front door while brushing dirt from his pants and elbows. "Hi, I'm Chet Collins, a forensic scientist. Did Watson explain my presence?"

The officer was familiar with the scene, and he waited to deliver the bones to the office. Digger advises he'll make contact tomorrow about the bones and whatever investigation might transpire because of them.

Once the bags rested in the vehicle, Digger walks over to the car where Ellie sits. He sees her on a phone call, enjoying the conversation. Detective Beck's name enters Digger's mind first. He sighs before touching the door handle.

Watson approaches. "We'll talk tomorrow about today's scenes. Have a good evening, and thanks again for your help. It's good to see you both."

"Same here, Watson." Digger opens the car door and slides into the seat. Ellie ends her call quickly without a glance towards Digger. She throws her hand up at Watson in a half-hearted wave.

"Are you ready to head home?" Digger asks, trying to sound chipper as his guts twist inside out. It's strange having stirred emotions over a female.

"Sure." Ellie starts the car and pulls out of the subdivision without another word. She acts as if she's concentrating on driving, but her mind is on other things.

Digger needs answers. He can't wait any longer. "Want to share about Detective Beck? I saw the look you two shared."

Chapter 3

Ellie clears her throat before beginning. "It was years ago. We were recent academy graduates and paired for a homicide investigation. The case spurred me into studying blood spatter. The killer was a guy getting back at his ex-girlfriend and her family. He butchered the girl's family, for lack of a better word, to death. She found her parent's bodies and ran to a neighbor's house for help. The neighbor called the police, and they assigned the investigation to Beck and me. We arrested the boy, but he pled not guilty. The girl testified against him, and along with our evidence, they sentenced him to death. Once the case ended, the girl killed herself in the living room of her old house in the same place he murdered her parents."

Digger shakes his head. "I'm sorry for bringing up such a horrific memory."

"Apology accepted, even though it wasn't necessary. You didn't know about the event. Detective Beck and I dated a few times after we closed it, but our careers got in the way." Ellie shrugs her shoulders as she focuses on the road ahead.

"I get it. In the past, my career took precedence over relationships, too. I'm hoping to remedy that now." Digger takes Ellie's hand in his and kisses the back of it. "Let's get back to your place for a shower."

They drive in silence, each thinking about the case and Detective Beck. Digger won't admit Detective

Beck disturbs him, and Ellie refuses to accept she's glad to see Beck again.

Once back in Ellie's house, Digger showers while Ellie searches for Beck's email. Her face has worry lines etched into it. "What's wrong, Ellie?" Digger asks when he sees Ellie's expression.

"Beck's email isn't in my inbox. I wanted to look at it to compare it with the other scene. Digger, these scenes are eerily similar. But the locations are a distance apart, not lending to the same killer."

Digger walks up behind Ellie and wraps her in a hug. "How about a pleasant dinner so we can relax? We can study the cases tomorrow. I have to contact the medical examiner to discuss the bones, anyway."

"I like it. Give me a minute to freshen up." Ellie turns and glides down the hallway.

While waiting for Ellie, Digger studies the photos from Ellie's first scene. He flips back to the carving. As he turns the picture around, the carving makes little sense. Maybe the killer is carving random shapes to throw the police off the investigation. There is potential for the carvings to mean nothing, but somehow, Digger disagrees.

Ellie and Digger enjoy the night with dinner and a stroll along the river. They talk and share about their childhoods and what their futures might bring. The evening brought about revelations of their feelings for each other but nothing further than acknowledgment.

Digger woke the following day to the smell of bacon and coffee. He rolls over to check the time on his phone, and he jumps straight up out of bed, tripping on his shoes as he opens the door. "Why didn't you wake me? I haven't slept this late in years."

"I peeked in on you, and I couldn't bring myself to disturb you. You were sleeping so soundly, and you had the cutest grin on your face." Ellie smiles as she remembers the look on his face.

Ellie piles a dish full of bacon, draws the biscuits out of the oven, and pours two mugs of coffee with ease. "Join me, Digger?"

Without a word, Digger strides to the table and takes a seat. After the first bite, he exclaims, "This is delicious. I didn't know you could cook too!"

"I tinker in the kitchen more than cook. It's therapeutic when I need to chill. If a case bothers me, I go to the kitchen and make stuff. It helps shift my thinking. Then when I review it again, I see things I couldn't before."

Digger nods as he understands. He removes himself from situations too to find the tiniest detail. "Thanks for breakfast. It was outstanding. Where should we start today?"

Ellie ponders the question, not sure where to start. "I'll check my email for the latest file. You call the Pittsburgh medical examiner and follow up on the bones. Then we regroup."

Both separate at the table, taking dishes to the kitchen. Digger volunteers to clean while Ellie prepares herself for the day. Her kitchen is tidy, as everything has a place. Just the way Digger likes things. The more he finds out about Ellie, the more he loves her. Although, he continues to question himself about living with another person. He hasn't shared a home with anyone in so long, and he wonders if he can.

With the kitchen spotless, Digger takes a seat on the sofa and calls the medical examiner's office. He enjoys music while the receptionist locates him. Once the examiner answers, they discuss the estimated time frame the buried bones were in the dirt. During the exam, the medical examiner determines they buried two skeletons years before the others. No identification yet. The teeth haven't turned up anything, and the skeletons have no broken bones to track. All four skeletons have no identifiable marks for the cause of death, either, although he found anomalies around the ear canals. Digger asks if he can look at them sometime today. The medical examiner welcomes the help. If Ellie doesn't want to make the trip again, he will find a rental car. He's traveling home tomorrow, anyway, so he could drop it at the airport.

Ellie comes into the family room with her phone touching her ear. She discusses the case with someone, and Digger has a nagging suspicion who it might be. He studies Ellie's expression while she listens. No signs suggest she's interested in this guy again. With the call over, Ellie asks Digger to join her at her desk for a case review.

They sit side by side at her desk, and Digger leans in and plants a kiss on her cheek. Ellie turns and kisses him. They giggle, then shift back to business.

Detective Beck is comprehensive in his files. When you finished reading his records, there were no unanswered questions about the scene. Beck included tons of photos too. Only one question remains, who is the killer?

The printer jumps to life as Ellie prints the file. Then she moves on to the photos. She prints these on glossy photo paper. With the two files and the scene pictures, we move to the other side of the room. We divide the whiteboard in half, allowing each case space. They discuss the similarities between them and jot down the points on the board. At the end of the comparison, they step back and then glance at each other.

A cell phone rings somewhere in the office. "that's my phone, Digger, but I can't find it."

Digger scoops it out from under a stack of paper. He notices the caller ID, Detective Marshall Beck. His insides quiver as he passes the phone to Ellie. He acts as if he's studying the board while eavesdropping on the conversation. Beck called with more information.

Ellie turns her phone to the speakerphone so Digger can hear Beck too. Beck learns of more murders with the same factors as theirs, and he requested all the case files from different districts in Pennsylvania. Detective Beck goes on record, stating they have a serial killer working in and around the Pittsburgh area.

Both heads turn together, and they agree with Beck's findings. Ellie calls Agent Watson and updates him. She explains what transpired this morning with the two files. Detective Beck requests a photo of their whiteboard, and he wants to work as a lead detective with Special Agent Watson. Beck asks Ellie to approach Watson with his idea.

After the call concludes, Ellie turns to Digger. "What are we going to say if Watson puts us on the case?"

"I'm working the bones case with the medical examiner already, and I'm meeting him this afternoon to look at the bones. The murders might be a coincidence, but I wouldn't mind being around for it. The bones are another case of an undetermined cause of death. Someone buried two skeletons long before the second set. This is odd too. I'd like for you to accompany me, but I understand if you had rather not."

Ellie grabs the files and asks, "what are we waiting on? I'd like a peek at them too."

The trip to the medical examiner's office was quick. Sundays are a leisure day for most people, but not for them. They had two investigations working, and Digger plans to leave tomorrow, so he's unsure how much help he can give the medical examiner. However, he wants to see the bones, anyway. For two hours, he examines the bones and the skulls. He confirms the anomalies around the ear canal. Then, he snaps photos of the bones, skulls, and the unexplained areas around the ear canal. Before leaving the building, Digger requests high-intensity x-rays for the skulls because he has a hunch. The medical examiner didn't question the request. The results will take a few hours, and Digger suggests he call when they're ready.

Ellie dials Watson, updating him on the case, while Digger shares an update on the bones. She gently approaches the subject of Detective Beck taking the lead on the serial killer. Ellie is unsure she wants to continue a close working relationship with Beck, given their past. Watson stammers before agreeing with Ellie, but he points out that Detective Larkin will be a part of the team. Ellie and Digger will remain consultants.

On the ride back to Ellie's house, Ellie and Digger discuss the cases. "What's your schedule over the next few weeks?" Digger inquires while reviewing Beck's file.

"I have a lecture in Maryland in two days, and that is all I know right now. My calendar is on my phone. Are you available if Watson calls us into working with them?"

"My teaching schedule is the most troublesome to move around, but Watson can call the college like he did last time. No one questioned me about my involvement. I've considered giving up the consultant gig to concentrate on my teaching, but investigations interest me. However, I don't want to neglect my students. Some of them signed up for my class because I'm the teacher. Only to find out I leave in the middle of semesters to help the FBI."

"Digger, I didn't know you were thinking about stepping aside, and I agree, that's a hard situation. You shouldn't have to choose between students or the FBI. Let the students know you might get whisked off somewhere, and they decide to take your class or not."

There was no response from Digger. His mind works overtime, thinking about Ellie's statement. Could he put a disclaimer on the bottom of his course offerings about the FBI? Would students still sign up for his classes? He likes the idea and will discuss it with his faculty.

"I hadn't considered your option, Ellie. I'll discuss the idea of a course disclaimer regarding the FBI. Then if the students decide to sign up, it would be their choice, and I shouldn't worry." Digger glances at Ellie with a grin since the outcome satisfies him.

As they pull into the parking lot, Digger's phone rings. Everything turns quiet as Digger listens to the Medical Examiner. "So, the x-rays highlight traces of lead particles in all four skulls. With the anomalies at the ear canal, I surmise someone shot the victims in the ear with a 22-caliber handgun. The caliber is small enough not to cause much damage. If they haven't demolished the house, we need a team to sift the crawl space for bullet fragments. I found none, but there is plenty of space left to search. Let me know."

"Did you hear the results of the x-rays?" Digger asks Ellie.

"I did. Why would a killer shoot someone in the ear? The ear is a strange place." Ellie wrinkles her nose as she considers her question.

"A small caliber bullet won't leave much damage making the cause of death more difficult to find. Come on. It's time to sort through today's recent information." Digger prepares his things to leave first thing in the morning. Ellie walks into his room and sits in the chair while he folds his clothes. "You know you don't have to leave so soon, right? We could travel to my lecture together."

"Tomorrow afternoon is test day. I need to be there for my students. Besides, I'm out of clean clothes. I didn't plan on jumping into the middle of two FBI investigations. Although it's not so bad with you by my side." Digger reaches for Ellie, and she stands and melts into his arms.

She loves the way she feels when he hugs her. It makes her feel protected and loved. Ellie hasn't felt protected since Montana. Digger saved her life after the knife attack, and then he stayed at the hospital with her. Maybe they can work things out for a future together.

Just as they were sitting down to a pleasant candlelight dinner, Ellie's phone rings. She answers without checking the caller ID. "Hi, Detective Beck.

Yes, Digger, oh sorry, I mean Chet. I'll place the call on speakerphone. We're both here."

"Hey guys, I hope I'm not interrupting. Chet, your nickname is Digger. I need to hear the back story on that one. Anyway, big developments this afternoon. I searched the state database of unsolved murders, and we have three or four more matches for our killer's MO. Once I receive them, I'll forward them to Ellie's email. If you get a chance, can you both look at these and see if you agree they belong in our group?"

"Sure, Beck. Send them on." The call ends, and Digger turns to Ellie. "All odds are in favor of a serial killer lurking in Pennsylvania. Watson suspects this outcome."

Ellie shakes her head. "I was hoping this wouldn't turn out to be a serial, but with the wounds on the chest, I suspected it too. The killer is drawing a picture using one person at a time as a canvas."

Dinner was somber as Ellie and Digger contemplated Beck's words. More unsolved murders, more carvings, and the lists continue. The conversation comprises their next visit. Their time spent together is minimal, so they try to find new places to visit while together. It's all about making memories.

Email alerts remind the pair of pending business. Once the kitchen is clean, they move to the office. The first email is from Watson, confirming the task force. The second email is from Beck, with four files attached. In the email's body, Beck mentions a murder investigation he had from a while back. Someone carved a quarter-size dot into the victim's chest on the breastbone. He admits this murder didn't come to mind until the search, and it remains unsolved.

Over the next hour, the duo prints files and assembles them in stacks. They begin the tedious chore of reviewing each file. Since the whiteboard is not large enough for all the cases, they turn to old-fashion paper.

In their late teens or early twenties, the victims are bound to a table or chair and gagged. Although, one victim was not. All had carvings in the chest. Ellie and Digger continue sifting through the information until the last case. As if on cue, they lean back in their chairs and sigh. Without a discussion, Ellie dials Beck. "They hold similarities, including yours. Your unsolved murder might have been the beginning for the murderer. The killer is drawing a picture of what we're uncertain about. Digger is leaving early in the morning, and I'm traveling to northern Maryland for a lecture." Beck thanks them for their input.

The sun had long since set, and their minds and bodies tired. Both need rest to face tomorrow. Digger takes hold of Ellie's hand. "When these are over, we'll have a serious talk about our future. Think hard about what you want. I already know my wants, but I realize it will cause changes in our lives." Digger leans in and kisses Ellie. They walk silently to their rooms.

Morning always comes sooner when you want the night to last. Digger steps out of his room with his suitcase in hand. Ellie stands at the window, sipping coffee. He walks over and plants a kiss on her neck. Ellie cannot beg, but she isn't ready to let this man walk out her front door. "Digger, I have enjoyed our time together, and I hate to see it end. Next time we visit, no murder or bone investigation will interfere."

"I can only hope you're right. At least we get the chance to work the investigations together. I need to get going if I want to make my flight." Digger kisses Ellie and bids her farewell. "I'll text as soon as I hit the tarmac." He walks out the door and turns back for one more look before stepping into his Uber.

Ellie turns back to the view from the window. Her mind swings from Digger to the murders. She needs to prepare for her speech tomorrow, and the planning has yet to begin.

Digger arrives on time, and so does his student testing. Except Watson interrupts class with a phone call, which turns into a three-way call with Ellie. Watson requests their presence in Pennsylvania for the murder investigation. Bob is flying into Pittsburgh today to help coordinate the task force. Ellie shares her schedule, including her lecture and travel time. She won't arrive until tomorrow afternoon. Digger confirms he'll make the trip tonight, after class, if he can secure a flight. Then he informs Watson and Ellie he'll work on the bones tomorrow while Ellie finishes her lecture. Bob will wait at the airport for Digger, and Ellie will drive up after the conference.

Things are rushing for Ellie and Digger. Ellie's concentration is lacking in her lecture topic. She changes course and decides on blood spatter again. The good news is this is her first time speaking at this school. She can talk about anything, and it will be new to them. Since she's driving, she can take her file copies. They might come in useful during the investigation.

Digger calls Detective Larkin on his way to the airport and advises him on the alternative plan. Larkin updates Digger and explains he's struggling to locate the owners. Gerald and Opal Teeter own the home. No one paid the property taxes on the house for fifteen years, and their bank accounts sit without action for close to fifteen years. The government continues to deposit their social security checks monthly as their money accrues. Both driver's licenses have expired, along with the insurance on the home and a vehicle. The vehicle's whereabouts are unknown too. No one had re-titled or tagged the car.

Since Larkin can't find the owners, he tracks down an old neighbor of the Teeter's. Their neighbor thought the Teeter's moved with the lack of work since the steel unions were in trouble. The Teeter's had a son, but he got himself mixed up in gangs, and the boy stopped coming by the house a long time ago. The neighbor doesn't remember the son's name.

With information from the neighbor, Larkin checks vital statistics, and Opal Teeter bore no children. He finds that interesting. So, he checks for Gerald as the father and nothing. How can the Teeter's have a son and no birth certificate? The adoption is next. Larkin explains his chase on the adoption angle, and it turns up dead too.

Digger can hear the frustration in Larkin's voice. "What about a death certificate for either?"

"Hold the line, Digger. I'll search." Digger listens as Larkin taps on his keyboard and waits for the results. "Nothing. Nada. Digger, this is weird. With no record of a son, no death certificate, and social security benefits still intact, what're your thoughts on it?"

A pause before Digger replies, "the two oldest skeletons in the crawl space will be the Teeter's. I have no answer for the other two."

Chapter 4

"What? How did you conclude that?"

"Well, Larkin, you rattled off a list of reasons. Just think about it. Draw a timeline from the presumed death of the bodies, the last time anyone saw them, the last time they touched their bank account, and let me know what you find. I've reached the airport parking. We'll meet in Pittsburgh."

On the plane, Digger scribbles ideas on a notepad. The second set of skeletons puzzles him. He can't fathom an identity. Did anyone else live in the house? Was it rented? If the original set turns out to be the Teeter's, the police could locate the family doctor and determine the next of kin. He highlighted that idea to share with Larkin. It's a shame they sold the neighborhood to accommodate the interstate system. Some other neighbors might have had some additional information.

The touchdown was uneventful, but Digger was eager to disembark. He still hates flying. As he headed for the baggage claim area, he wiped the sweat shine from his face, then he continued at a steady pace. When he rounded the corner, Bob stood at the luggage carousel with a sign that simply read, 'Digger.' He waves when he sees Digger.

Digger and Bob greet one another with handshakes. Bob plucked Digger's luggage from the rack before he arrived. "How's it going, Bob?"

"Good. It looks like we'll work together on another serial killer investigation. Your room is ready at the hotel, and the others are waiting for us. I hear Ellie will join us tomorrow?"

"You heard correct. She's giving a lecture in the morning and will arrive tomorrow afternoon. Which works out for me since I need to spend time with Detective Larkin on the bones."

"Our car is at the curb. I'm ready if you are."

The men climb into the black Suburban and hit the highway. Bob makes an exceptional driver, which allows Digger time to call Larkin. "Larkin, Digger here. I'm on my way to the hotel. Did the medical examiner confirm the identity of the first skeletons?" Digger pauses while Larkin speaks.

"I was hoping to hear something today. If it turns out to be the Teeter's, maybe we could gather some information from the family doctor if we can find them. See you soon."

Digger sighs as he leans back in the seat. Bob didn't disturb him because he knows Digger well enough to know when he ponders ideas. The muscles in his jaw move, and the veins at his temples pop out. Something bothers Digger.

After sufficient time, Bob breaks the silence. "What's your take on the killings, Digger?"

"I have two investigations running simultaneously. Ellie let me tag along to a murder scene Watson asked her to visit, and while there, Watson steered me to another scene involving bone discovery. Both cases are odd. Ellie's killer carves pictures into their victim's chest and stomach, and my bones are unidentifiable. The bones were in a crawl space of a home slated for demolition. Gerald and Opal Teeter owned the residence. No one has seen them in years. One neighbor thought they moved away when work became scarce. The weird part of it is the bank is holding a boatload of untouched money from their social security benefits."

"I didn't realize you had a separate case from Ellie. This situation is a little strange. You're working with Detective Larkin on the bones. Who's working with the serial killer?"

Digger squirms in his seat because Detective Beck gets under his skin, but he tries not to show it. "Detective Marshall Beck from Pittsburgh is the lead detective on the killer. Detective Larkin is also a part of the task force. In Ellie's first scene, she told Larkin they were looking for a serial killer. No other reason for the carving. Beck found other cases in the state with similarities. The task force is meeting tomorrow afternoon to discuss them."

Bob nods his head as he digests the information. What are the odds of these two cases running simultaneously in the same city? Tomorrow will be interesting. After all his years at the FBI, serial killers still fascinate Bob. His college thesis was about the mind of a serial killer. What made the killer chose his method? How does a killer select their victims?

The hotel was ready for the crew. Watson met the men in the lobby, and then they slipped off for a bite. It's nice to catch up with friends. Afterward, Digger went to his room. While thinking, he doodled as his mind worked on scenarios for both crimes. The question that bothers him the most is who are the skeletons in the crawl space?

Larkin meets Digger for breakfast the following day. They discuss the crime scene, bones, and the possible identity of the skeletons. Digger's first thought is the Teeter's, but he still doesn't guess the second set of skeletons. After several scenarios, Larkin agrees with Digger since he bases his idea on the known information. The medical examiner requests a meeting this morning at his office. So they load the vehicle after the meal and drive into the city.

Today is a gorgeous spring day with a slight breeze and wispy white clouds in the sky. It would have been a pleasant day to walk along the river with Ellie. The sun would bring out the highlights in her hair, and she would look as if she were glowing. It's times like these Digger can't concentrate on anything but Ellie.

The medical examiner's office sits in the basement of police headquarters. Over the years, with the population growth, the office expanded its footprint by taking over file rooms. They moved the paper files to an offsite storage building since they now store most records in the cloud. They renovated portions of the lab and office space with the expansion by adding advanced blood analysis machines. Larkin leads the way to the basement through the back door. The only way to gain entry is with an ID card.

"Does the morgue have another entrance? It seems awkward to swipe a card for entrance, and the public has no way inside." Digger questions as he surveys the area.

"Public access is through the front, which is inside the lobby of police headquarters. The police use this door so that we can miss the metal detectors and such."

Digger nods, accepting the reply. He whistles when he enters, showing admiration for the polished look of the medical examiner's office. "If this is the back entrance, I can't wait to see the front. The floors glisten without a speck of dust."

Their arrival didn't go unnoticed as the lead medical examiner met them at the door. "Welcome, gentlemen. Follow me, please. The skeletons are ready for your visual inspection if you so desire. I would like to take this opportunity to point out something to Chet."

"Show me what you have. I hope its wonderful news."

The medical examiner walks to the first metal table and turns the bright light onto the victim, showing an incomplete skeleton. He explains several leg bones are missing. These skeletons were in the dirt for approximately fifteen years—the other two around ten years ago.

"I think both pairs of skeletons are a man and a woman. I guessed the identity of the first set." Digger offers.

"I agree, and I wanted to share that bit of news and advise you all skeletons have the same anomalies at the ear canal. I surmise the killer shot each victim in the ear with a small-caliber weapon. Of course, I can't confirm the caliber without a bullet fragment, but each skull has lead traces inside. I'd like to hear your guess for the first set of skeletons."

Larkin speaks, "Gerald and Opal Teeter were the homeowners where the demolition crew found the bones. There is no record of them for the last fifteen years. Their social security benefits continue with a monthly deposit into an account at a local bank. No one has attempted to take the money. It's like they vanished."

The medical examiner pauses a second. "I'll ask an assistant to search for their family doctor and check into hospital visits. If we can find that, we can identify two skeletons and have only two remaining."

After the visit, Larkin and Digger walk to the elevator. Both thinking about the victims. Why would someone bury them in the crawl space of their own home? Didn't they have friends or family looking for them?

Larkin enters the elevator first then shares. "We need to check on the possibility of the Teeter's owning a gun. The killer could have stolen the gun from the Teeter's and shot them with it."

"The only way to find out is to run a check on them. I can't get over the idea of a son floating around without records to support it. There is no child or relative listed on the bank account. Did you check into the social security benefits? They should have listed a beneficiary."

"Splendid idea, Digger. I didn't check when I found out there were no children in vital records. I'll run a firearm and social security check when we get to the office. The task force is meeting this afternoon. Ellie told Watson she would arrive after lunch."

The men arrive in a flurry of activity. People are in and out of the conference room with whiteboards and a huge Pennsylvania state map. They are preparing the place for the task force meeting. Digger's excitement kicked up a notch when he thought how close he was to seeing Ellie.

Larkin points to a chair at the end of his desk for Digger. He powers on his computer and begins keying information. Within minutes, he reports on the Teeter's. Opal Teeter was the proud owner of a 22-caliber handgun.

"Well, well. Her gun could be our murder weapon. What about the beneficiary?" Digger nodded.

"Hold on. The report doesn't list a beneficiary other than the Teeter's. So, they are the beneficiaries of each other's. So, that leaves another question. Is there no other family living? Doesn't it seem strange?"

"We haven't solved it yet. But we will." Digger admits as he shakes his head. "Critical information is missing, but we'll find it in time. Was the Teeter's gun ever reported stolen?"

"Not according to the report. Opal is still the listed owner. That brings up another question. Who disposed of the Teeter's contents if no family came forward?"

"Another good question, Larkin. Whoever set the demolition in motion should have a record of the disposal unless someone removed the contents before the government condemned the property. But who that person is, I have no clue."

Watson walks over to Digger and shakes his hand. "Nice to see you again, Digger. Any progress on the bones?"

Digger and Larkin update Watson on the known facts. Watson's eyebrows lift when the men explain their idea of the first set of skeletons identities. After the explanation, his eyebrows bunch together while Watson works through the scenario. "You said there are no death certificates for Gerald or Opal Teeter nor birth records for them either. What gave you the possibility of the Teeter's?"

"Process of elimination gave us the idea. No one has paid the property taxes on the Teeter's home for fifteen years. The bank accounts are untouched for fifteen years, no driver's license renewals, no car insurance registered with the state for the same time. It led us to believe the Teeter's are the first set of skeletons. The timeline fits."

"It sounds like you might be right. If the deceased isn't in the system, the identification falls to the medical examiner. I'm assuming you had this conversation with him."

"Yes, we spoke with him this morning, and he has a team on it. We might get lucky and know for certain within a few days." Digger said as his eyes moved to the doorway. There, in the middle, is Ellie. Her eyes meet his, and she walks to him.

They embrace for a moment while the other task force members enter the surrounding room. Digger whispers to Ellie how happy he is to see her, and he watches as she blushes. She takes a seat next to him and Watson. Bob squeezes her shoulder as he plops down into the chair beside Watson. It feels good to be in the company of these men. Ellie has nothing but admiration for them and what they do day in and day out.

Detective Marshall Beck strides into the room, holding a box full of files. He turns and faces the group, and his eyes land on Ellie's. The task force members know how Beck feels about her. Ellie turns her head toward Watson when he asks her a question about her trip. Watson diverts a showdown, at least this time, as he watches Digger out of the corner of his eye. Watson jots a reminder to himself to mention to Beck about Ellie and Digger's relationship. The task force doesn't need a love interest impeding the capture of a killer.

Introductions fly around the room. Someone taped a map to the wall, and pushpins showcased the murders. The city has scattered murders, from north to south and east to west. So, where does the killer live, and how does he decide on his victims?

Ellie stares at the map as she ponders each location of the murders while Beck takes a call. His face is deep red, and now he appears ready to explode when he faces them. When the call ends, he walks out of the room for a few minutes, gathering his wits. Our meeting begins with Beck advising the group of a recent murder. However, no one notified the task force because of irregularities, but the medical examiner called when he found a carving in the victim's belly. The carving is a straight line from the middle of the stomach to the side. This murder occurred near Larimer. Beck walks over to the map and adds a pushpin as he explains the file is being compiled and forwarded.

"This meeting will be lengthy. Coffee and snacks are available on the back table. Get up and walk around if you have a need. FBI Special Agent Watson is catering supper for us. Cancel your evening plans now. We'll begin in fifteen minutes."

With everyone seated around the table, the meeting starts. Beck instructs the group to interrupt with questions as he outlines each murder scene. He begins with his murder investigation from a month ago. The victim is Asian in his late teens or early twenties, and he lived in a rundown duplex on the outskirts of town. The killer shot the victim in the head while seated in the family room and then drug him to the kitchen, where the killer tied him to a kitchen table leg. There is a small circle carved into the center of his breastbone. At first glance, it looked as if it was a burn. The medical examiner confirms the carved circle occurred after death. There are no suspects, no witnesses, and no DNA. The victim has an arrest record for theft and burglary with a weapon.

The second murder occurred eight months ago outside of Harrisburg. This victim is Caucasian, late teens, and he lived alone in a mobile home. The police arrested him for drug possession and distribution, disorderly conduct with alcohol. The killer shot the victim at the front door, and he fell onto the carpet. Then he moved him to the kitchen, but since there was no kitchen table, the killer placed him in the only seat in the house, a ragged recliner. The medical examiner's office found the carving, as it was hard to spot in the guy's tattoos. The carving is on the breastbone and is a rectangle sitting on its small end. It is the size of a man's first thumb joint. But, again, there are no suspects, witnesses, or DNA.

Beck stops and asks the group if they have questions. He prepares his laptop with the third murder, and photos pop up on the wall showing the crime scene. This victim is of Spanish descent. He lived in an apartment in a neighborhood north of the city. So far, all the murders have occurred in the Pittsburgh suburbs. The victim has two arrests for DUI, and a third arrest was DUI with drug possession and distribution. He is a clean-cut guy in his early twenties, with no tattoos and short hair. His carving is visible on the right side of his chest.

It is a line with an upward curl on end. Someone bound and gagged the victim to a kitchen chair. He suffered two shots at close range in the head, and this is the first murder where a neighbor offered information. The neighbor stated to the police he heard two guys yelling, but no one called the police.

After no one stops Beck, he continues into the fourth murder. He announces Ellie's role in this crime scene. We have a young, black male victim with tattoos and gang marks. He lived alone in an apartment to the east of Pittsburgh. The killer also tied him to a kitchen chair, and they used a headscarf to gag him. They shot the victim twice in the head at close range. He was dead twenty-four hours before someone found him. The killer carved a picture of a straight line with an upward curl on the left side of the victim's chest. Again, no suspects and no witnesses.

Detective Beck asks Ellie to share her observations of the scene. Her view of the scene begins with the blood spatter around the table area. She explains blood spatter in layperson's terms as best as she can. Multiple drops land on other drops, and she points out the space in the blood spatter. This proves the shooter's location at the time of the crime. Ellie tells the group they are looking for a left-handed shooter and carver. Again, pointing to the photos, she emphasizes the blood in the next room, and the drops show the shooter shook his hand off, trying to rid himself of blood. The shooter would have had traces of blood on his clothes and skin. Larkin added the victim spent time in jail for theft, burglary, and robbery. His latest conviction was a home invasion.

Beck retakes the reins as no one asks questions. He's unsure about the lack of talking amongst the group since crime scenes always bear questions. Shaking it off, he describes murder five. Another young Caucasian male in his early twenties was shot and killed in his two-bedroom, one-bath home west of Beltzhoover. The killer tied the victim to a dining room column, as there is no furniture in the kitchen and only a fold-out sofa and television in the den. A potential renter peeked through the blinds, saw a person's foot. They notified the landlord, and the landlord called us. Someone carved a straight line from just under the breastbone to the naval into the victim's chest.

Detective Campagna raises his hand. "Ellie, were you at this scene? You provided valuable information on the other scene."

Ellie shook her head no. "I was at a speaking engagement during this murder. However, I saw the next one."

Beck describes this scene while staring at Ellie. She shifts in her chair, trying to break the stare. Finally, Beck looks away. Digger notices Ellie is uncomfortable and reaches for her hand and gently squeezes it for reassurance.

The next scene was where Ellie and Digger joined the crew. This victim is Asian, and he worked at an eatery. He lived in an apartment on the backside of the complex. His co-worker found the deceased when he didn't show for work. His arrest record showed multiple arrests for burglarizing and robbing liquor stores. The victim was bound and gagged with a straight line carved into the left side of his stomach, just above the naval. After this scene, FBI Special Agent Watson sent out a statewide alert for other murders with the same attributes.

Someone discovered the latest murder this morning. The victim was in an upstairs apartment, and something must have spooked the killer because he shot the victim through a pillow. The victim wasn't tied or gagged, either. There was no furniture in the apartment, only floor pillows. Because of the irregularities, no one notified the task force of this murder. The medical examiner's office discovered another carving of a straight line on the right side of the belly, and they called Beck when they found the carving.

"So, as of now, we have seven murders with the same MO. Someone carved a picture or a symbol into the victim, and they all happened in the Pittsburgh area. Does anyone have questions?"

Digger raises his hand with a puzzled expression. "Do we know the caliber of bullet used in the shootings?"

Chapter 5

Beck glances at his notes, then he says, ".22-caliber handgun."

Larkin sucks in a breath as he shares a glance with Digger. Could they be searching for the same killer? Then Larkin speaks, "do we have slugs for comparisons?"

"Yes. I'll have to pull the information to let you know the total, but we have several that match other bullets." Beck explains.

Digger waves it off. "The total isn't necessary. We just want clarification. If we find the gun, we can match the bullets." Digger's head spins, given the last bit of information.

Watson stands and advises everyone to take a break, reminding them of the coffee and snacks. Then Watson leans over to Digger, Larkin, and Ellie and invites them into the hallway for a quick discussion. "What's up with the questions, Digger? Do you think the bones relate to the murders?"

"It's a strong possibility. Mrs. Teeter owned a 22-caliber handgun. What are the odds? The Teeter's lived east of Pittsburgh too. The same area as the first murder. Just an idea to investigate at some point."

Larkin and Ellie agree with Digger. There are too many coincidences for the cases to be unrelated. Ellie asks, "Did the medical examiner find out the identity of the other set of bones?"

"Not yet," Larkin said with his head down. "This will interest us if it turns out I'm working two cases with one killer. That's never happened to me before."

Beck calls everyone back to the conference room. He wants to set the stage for the investigation and assign teams. There will be five or six teams of two, and if we need more, we'll get more. Watson and Bob, both FBI, will be a team. Next are Larkin and Digger. Beck continues down the line, ending with his partner being Ellie. Watson looks at Ellie and shakes his head no.

Ellie is unsure she can continue working with Beck. She thought they could have a professional relationship. Since they last saw each other at the crime scene, he hasn't called or mentioned their relationship. But his stares are unsettling. Ellie doesn't want to run away from helping someone, but she can't concentrate while worrying about her co-worker. Watson seems to understand her predicament. Once Watson speaks with Beck, maybe he'll give up the staring contest.

Beck gives Ellie the cold shoulder after his discussion with Watson. With her group standing around her, Ellie states, "Guys, I'm unsure if I should work this serial killer case. Tension is running high between Beck and myself, and it shouldn't affect the outcome of the investigation."

Watson speaks in an authoritative tone, "If Beck wants to keep his current position, he'll need an attitude change. I was unaware of your past relationship, but I would assume past feelings were dead after this many years. The FBI chooses the team for serial murder cases. Beck's reputation is flawless in his police career, but I'm sure Larkin can fill his shoes. Ellie, I want you on this case. You have already given us pertinent information on the shooter."

Digger and Larkin nod their heads in unison. "How about we grab supper, then have a night to rest, and we'll start fresh in the morning?" Larkin suggests, and the group agrees.

Bob drives the group to the nearest steak house. The aroma is mouthwatering, and the meal is enjoyable. Ellie doesn't worry about Beck as she relaxes. Instead, they speak of the murders in between server visits. Ellie questions the group about the shooter. "What are the odds the victims were in prison at the same time?"

"Prison is a distinct possibility. Larkin, can you pull those records for us? We can check on this tomorrow."

Larkin jots a note in his notebook as a reminder. "Sure can, Digger. Prison information is easy to find."

After the day ends, the group splits into their hotel rooms. Ellie remains apprehensive about staying in a hotel room, even though she has done it since the accident. The memories flood her brain, and she can't turn them off. Being stabbed is one thing but being stabbed by a serial killer takes on a whole new meaning. The stabbing left an unsightly scar on her arm. Every so often, she considers reconstructive surgery, but the downtime remains a turnoff.

Ellie's hotel room is identical to the one where the stabbing took place. The closet doors are closed, and Ellie must work up the courage to open them. If she doesn't, she won't sleep. She should know because she's tried. She can only make it through the night by opening the closet doors because the serial killer, whose sights were on Ellie, hid in the hotel room closet before the attack.

The night progresses as Ellie responds to emails about lectures. When the time comes to lie down, Ellie always picks the bed farthest from the closet. Even with the doors wide open, sleep doesn't come easy. At midnight, Ellie gently taps on the connecting door.

Digger turns the lock on the door and opens it to see Ellie standing with a robe pulled tightly around her. "I can't sleep. Closets give me nightmares."

With a slight pull, Ellie walks into Digger's arms. Her body trembles as she lays her head on his shoulder. "Want to share a room? You can have the other bed, or if you feel more comfortable, we can leave the connecting door open." Digger looks into Ellie's eyes as he waits for an answer.

"As long as you sleep in the bed next to the closet, I'll stay." Ellie's eyes turn down as shades of pink flush her face. When she's embarrassed, she turns colors. Always has. Always will.

"Come on. We need to sleep. Tomorrow will be a long day." They walk into Digger's room hand in hand.

The following day, the sun shines bright. Ellie slips out of Digger's room before he awoke. She works on her laptop when Digger pops his head into her room. "What time did you wake? I didn't hear a thing." Digger asks.

"I slept so soundly. I woke early and used my time to work. As soon as you dress, we can head down for breakfast." Ellie pauses before she continues, "Thanks, Digger."

With a grin on his face, he bows and makes his way to the shower. Fifteen minutes later, they stand at the elevators waiting on the doors to open. The doors slide open and reveal Watson and Larkin standing in the back corners.

"Good morning, you two." Watson addresses Ellie and Digger. "We're stopping by the dining room for breakfast. I hope you plan on it too."

"Coffee is first, then food. Are we going to canvas the neighborhood?" Digger questions.

Watson addresses the group. "After breakfast, we're going to survey the scene and visit neighbors. Detective Campagna wants to meet us there. He says the area is busy with foot and road traffic. Someone should have heard something even if they saw nothing. I advised Campagna I'd call as soon as we're on our way."

Breakfast discussions center on the murders and Detective Beck. Watson tells the group he spoke with Beck last night, and Beck understands the situation. "I explained Digger and Ellie are a couple and hope you two didn't mind me sharing, but I thought it was in the best interest of everyone."

Larkin looks from Digger to Ellie and then to Watson. "Really? You two are dating. Outstanding. Congratulations, guys."

Ellie and Digger throw out thanks to Larkin, but Digger is unsure how to feel about the relationship being out in the open. They've kept it under wraps since they began dating. Ellie smiles as if it relieved her.

"I'm glad Beck is good with it. I didn't want to be the reason for a volatile work environment. Thanks, Watson, for handling the situation."

"Anytime, Ellie. Is everyone ready to hit the streets?" Watson asks.

As the group climbs into Larkin's vehicle, Watson's phone rings. After he answers, he raises his hand as if to say stop. Five minutes later, the call ends. "We have a change in plans. Detective Chavez called Beck, who called me. We have another murder, and this one is in a new area. It's another mobile home at the back of the park. I have the address. Chavez is holding the crime scene guys until we can get there."

Larkin sits behind the wheel while Watson slides into the passenger seat. Ellie and Digger share the back seat. With notebook in hand, Ellie jots down Watson's information, then leans back and prepares her mind for what she might see.

This is an older area with boarded-up buildings, and those not boarded have bars outside the windows. The streets are pothole-filled and have less asphalt than in other areas. Many people walk in this area with sidewalks on both sides of the road. The entrance sign to the mobile home park states it is the largest mobile home community on this side of the city.

Digger takes in the surroundings, too. He doesn't miss much when he's on a scene. There is more foliage around this park than most. People sit on logs under trees, and some are on lounge chairs. No one waves as the vehicle drives through. As a few men stand from their chairs, bulges protrude at their waist for gun placement.

"Some of these people carry firearms at their waistband. No one goes anywhere alone. We stay in pairs, no questions." Watson states firmly.

"I have no intention of leaving alone. These people have fierce looks on their faces. They must think we are trespassing or something." Ellie replies.

Larkin locates the mobile home at the back of the community next to the wood line. The house is older but somewhat lovely in this area. Chavez leans on his car as we pull into the parking area. "FBI Special Agent Watson, I am Detective Chavez. Nice to meet you."

Watson introduces the rest of his group, and Chavez leads us to the front door. "It's messy. There are booties and gloves on a table at the bottom of the stairs. So far, I've found out the victim rents this mobile home and has for the last several months. He spent some time in prison, but I don't have a clue for what yet. Once you see the scene, my guys will start the neighborhood canvas. I can only hope someone speaks up if they have information."

Ellie and Digger have the privilege of stepping into booties and pulling on gloves first. An officer opens the door to exit, and a whiff brushes across Ellie's nose. There's the smell. She gasps, then glances at Digger. "Ready?"

"Come on. The sooner we go in, the sooner we come out." Digger announces as he enters the house first. Through the doorway, you enter the family room. A two-foot vinyl square greets your entrance. Then some putrid-colored carpet picks up the floor covering from there. The kitchen is to the right, then bedrooms and baths are down a skinny hallway to the left. Our victim sat tied to a kitchen table leg with an old shirt. The carving is visible and is a tilted vertical line on the right side of the chest. Did the killer intend for the picture to be slanted further out on the bottom?

Ellie surveys the scene from the door. Her mind absorbs the sights as she processes the evidence. Digger stands where the killer stood. Ellie notices the amount of blood from the victim to the doorway. By her best guess, the victim's heart was still pumping when the carving started. Large blood droplets formed from the incision and hung down at an awkward angle. Blood clotting will help the medical examiner solve the time of death. A few of the drops appear to have little clotting.

Larkin walks over to Digger and Ellie. "Your thoughts, please. Ellie, you can go first."

With the gap in the blood spatter, Ellie points out the shooter's location. She also provides details about the blood drops from the incision and the idea of less clotting around the incision compared to the head wounds. The shooter also exited the same door as she pointed to drops that had dropped from his gun. Also, two strange blood patterns lead from the victim to the door. Ellie takes a photo of those. Then she walks over to the kitchen area behind the victim and studies an unfamiliar territory. Ellie stands and returns to the group.

Glancing at the men, Ellie says, "your turn, Digger."

"I have nothing on the blood, but I have one additional thing to add to the shooter."

The group looks at him with anticipation. "Well, Digger, what is it?"

"It's clear the victims know the shooter. The shooter knocks on the door, and the victims invite them inside. The killer ties them up and then kills them or vice versa. He might kill them, then tie them up. Either way, they know each other. With that in mind, we need to cross-reference the victim's records and see where the commonalities meet."

Watson nods his head in agreement. "We'll start on that after our next stop on the way back to the office."

The group walks to the car as Digger and Watson's cell phones ring. They answer their phones. Larkin and Ellie stroll to a shade tree near the edge of the mobile home. Ellie looks around the ground while Larkin writes in his notebook. "What is this, Larkin? It looks like blood." Ellie surmises.

"Let me grab a swab from the tech guys." Larkin bounds up the steps to retrieve the swab while Digger and Watson discuss business.

Larkin leans over and swabs the area Ellie found. He looks at it and says, "this is blood, Ellie. I'll place a marker beside it while you search for more."

The duo searches for blood on the dry-packed dirt drive. Chavez joins the search when they share their find. Ellie makes her way to the back of the mobile home when she spots more blood. "Over here, Larkin. And here is another."

Chavez raises his head and deciphers his location. "Look back there. We have a wood line. Could the shooter have walked through the woods? Wonder what's on the other side of the trees?"

Ellie and Larkin survey the area and then agree with Chavez. It's likely the shooter parked somewhere in the woods or close by and walked into the community. This confirms these murders are premeditated and not a crime of opportunity. Serial killers who go through all this trouble locating and planning out their attack are the most ruthless. Although the victims know the shooter, it's just a matter of time before the police catch them.

Chapter 6

The group walks toward the trees when they hear
Watson calling for them. Ellie waves, and Digger
and Watson join the hike. Chavez explains what led
them to the woods. The trees stand tall with budding
leaves and not much undergrowth yet. When the
weather changes and the nighttime temperature
stops its plummet, the undergrowth will have a
growth spurt. Sun shining through the branches
makes it easy to navigate, but the group watches
their footfalls since the ground is uneven.

"Look here, a road. It appears to be a long-lost road
too with no homes or businesses." Chavez states as
he pulls his phone out of his pocket. He touches the
app for GPS and then studies the result. "This road
doesn't exist on my GPS. How did the killer know
about it?"

Chavez looks up at everyone with a puzzled
expression on his face. "Can someone answer my
question? If GPS doesn't recognize the road, did the
shooter drive around until he found it, or has the
shooter driven it before? This shooter seems odd to
me."

"Either way is a possibility," Digger adds as he
surveys the area.

Watson looks both ways on the road, "Any chance
for tire marks?" Watson walks a little way, and then
he runs the toe of his shoe across the street, "I think
I answered my question. This road is packed hard. It
has no road signs either, so the state doesn't
maintain it. I'll follow up with the state DOT and

see if they know anything about it. We need to get to our next stop, then to the office."

The group trudges their way back to the car and is happy when they reach it. Larkin slides into the driver's seat. The rest follows and bids farewell to Chavez. The group discusses the latest scene, and their arrival at the new scene doesn't go unnoticed either. People watch the vehicle pass each intersection on its way to the apartment complex. The neighborhood has lots of unkept vacant yards bordering the streets. Ellie glances at Digger and takes hold of his hand. These scenes have the same characteristics. It must mean something.

Digger exits the vehicle first and surveys the area. He catches an older gentleman sitting on the steps, so Digger ambles over and strikes up a conversation with him. The man divulges what he knows about the shooting. A neighbor in the victim's building heard a muffled sound but didn't bother to check it. Another neighbor said he witnessed an unfamiliar guy walking down the stairs. The unknown guy was white, wearing dirty clothes, and he never raised his head. He kept his head down as he walked away.

Ellie jumps into the conversation and asks the neighbor, "did anyone mention a car?"

"No, they did not. The neighbor said he just walked away toward the road."

Digger looked at Ellie, and they thanked the older man for his time. They share their information with Larkin and Watson as they stride through the complex. Larkin points the way to the crime scene.

He produces a key and opens the apartment for the group. The group splits at the door, going separate ways. This apartment was a breeze to examine since it doesn't hold many personal items.

Ellie recalls the scene. "This victim wasn't bound or gagged. He was lying on the kitchen floor, but the blood spatter proved he was standing here when he took the bullets. The killer carved his picture where he fell. Was he in a hurry?"

"Maybe the sheer number of people in the apartment complex caused him to hurry. Maybe it spooked him." Digger adds.

Then Watson, "does our killer walk-in for the kill? Is he that deliberate? If he is, wonder what happens if we don't capture him before the picture is complete? Will he simply find another picture and start over?"

"Watson, we can't assume anything. We'll capture him before he finishes this picture. We're gaining on him, and we'll find the connection in the victim's records. All these people crossed paths somewhere. It's not luck he chose these victims."

Everyone shakes their heads, agreeing with Ellie. "Time to head to the office. This place isn't helping us. We have all the information we need from here."

The group endures another road trip to the office. Four people sure have unique ideas about crime scenes, but they agree to concentrate on the records in the end. If they can find a common thread, then the likelihood of finding this killer just jumped drastically.

The foursome walks into the conference room and into the path of Detective Beck. He greets them all, including Ellie, with respect. Each member greets him in return, and Beck requests an update. Everyone sits at the conference table and recites the recent information from the scenes. Beck perks up when he hears about the blood trail leading into the woods. "I've contemplated the killer's mode of transportation. When the shooter enters the victim's house, is his sole intention to murder the victim? If so, until we can find the common factor with the victims, this killer will be hard to capture."

Watson and Ellie exchange a glance. "Sounds like a repeat from someone else in the group," Ellie states with a snicker as she glances at Digger.

Larkin emphasizes, "we submitted the requests for the victim's backgrounds. We have an hour before they'll be ready. If we can find a commonality between the victims, we have our next target. Freshen up, get coffee, and meet back here in thirty minutes."

Everyone exits the room for a break and returns calls while they can. Ellie leans against a wall in the hallway when Beck saunters her way, and he listens to her conversation as it ends. "Hi, Ellie. I'm sorry for the misunderstanding earlier. I was unaware of your relationship with Digger. However, I would still like a few minutes with you just to catch up. It's been a long time since we've seen each other."

70

"Thanks, Marshall, for understanding. It was an awkward situation, for sure. We'll see about squeezing in some time to talk. The group is reconvening in the conference room to discuss the victim's background. Are you joining us?"

"After I return a call, I will," Beck replies. With his head down, he strolls away.

Ellie turns and walks into the conference room, ready to tackle the backgrounds. The men wait for her, and Digger suspects her delay. But, with Larkin at the helm, he begins with the backgrounds, and Digger doesn't get the chance to ask Ellie questions. Larkin passes out the reports like candy. Each has a murder report involving a carved victim. Larkin suggests everyone read their victims' background when their time comes, adding the information to the board.

The first point is each victim has an arrest record. The charges range from theft to drugs to home invasion. Next, all the victims spent time in jail and or prison, depending on the crime. The group proves the victims spent their jail time at different locations. They rule that idea out.

Frustration is apparent as the team gets nowhere with the backgrounds. "What are we missing? There must be something here." Watson expresses.

Bob suggests, "Has anyone considered the arresting officers or the parole officer as being the common denominator in this case?"

The team members share glances, and Digger replies, "now, why didn't I think of that?"

Paper rustles as the members search for the arresting officers first. Fifteen minutes later, Bob's idea is a bust. Different officers from across the state made arrests. Next, they moved on to the parole officer. Some background reports didn't list the parole officer, so Larkin calls for help.

Once they identified the parole officers, that idea is also a bust. "We're striking out all over the place. We have one parole officer, James Henderson, that has two of our victims. Maybe we should visit him tomorrow. James might help us."

"Which victims belong to James?" Ellie inquires.

Larkin pulls the list and answers, "Victim is Jeffrey Cooke. His murder was in the Harrisburg community almost a year ago. The second victim is Corbin Matthews, and his murder occurred near Beltzhoover. Did you see either of those scenes, Ellie?"

"No, I didn't. I was at a speaking engagement for the one near Beltzhoover. I almost forgot to show you a photo of a blood pattern. This pattern was inside the mobile home of the latest victim. I noticed as I walked out the door how the droplets had an odd shape. After some research, it appears the killer drug his shoes across the floor, or the killer wore long pants which touched the floor. Let me show you."

Ellie opens her laptop and turns it so the group can view it. She magnified the photo to emphasize her thoughts and waited for an acknowledgment.

Digger was first. "I see how you thought this odd. I'm not sure I would have put shoes and pants together to make these marks. But now that you point out, it makes sense, and it's an excellent catch."

"With this information, when we catch this killer, we need to remember to check his shoes and his closet for extra-long pants," Ellie states as she types a note to herself.

Larkin packs his files into his bag. "I say we call it a day. My ask of you is to ponder ways to connect the victims. We'll meet for breakfast, then jump back into the files. It's here. We just have to find it."

Bob drives the group to the hotel, and they decide to grab a sandwich in the bar. They have fallen in love with the hotel bar food. The bar sits in the back of the lobby with dark paneling and sparkling chandeliers. Booths surround the outside walls with round tables in the middle. All have black leather seating. Between the mirrors behind the bar and the black leather, the bar is stunning. No one would expect a hotel bar to carry these features.

After devouring a scrumptious burger, the group splits and heads to their rooms. Digger takes a spin in the fitness room while Ellie takes a hot bath. The brief encounter with Beck has had her in knots all day. She needs to relax, or she will never sleep tonight.

When Digger finishes his shower, he taps on the connecting door, and Ellie invites him into her room. He chuckles when he sees the case files spread out on the bed. "Do you ever stop? Your brain needs a break."

"I'll stop after this killer is behind bars. Will you help me out with something? I want to draw the picture the killer is carving into the victims."

"Sure. Are there enough pieces of the puzzle to determine the picture?"

Ellie peruses the files. "Probably not, but I want to see what we have so far."

After handing Digger a note card and a pen, she says, "I'll describe the carving, and you draw each one on a separate card. Then we'll lay them out like a puzzle and see if they fit."

With the note cards spread out on the round table by the window, Ellie and Digger stare at the pieces, shuffle them, and stare some more. Nothing comes to mind. "What are you thinking, Digger? Any ideas?"

"Not with the pieces we have. It makes little sense what this represents. I feel sure it means something to the killer, but what?"

After a few more minutes with the cards, Ellie shoves them out of the way. "We need to show these to the team tomorrow. They may pick up on something."

Digger takes Ellie's chin and lifts it upward. "Can you call it a day now? Please rest. I'll see you in the morning." Digger leans in and kisses Ellie goodnight and slips through the door. As soon as the door closes, Ellie hears the news channel. Digger loves his news shows.

Ellie lays her head back on the pillow, rehearsing her day. She hopes Beck decides against the meeting between them. There is no way she can meet Beck with Digger in the next room unless she slips out without his knowledge. Should she take the chance? She would like to hear the reason Beck stopped calling her all those years ago. She stands to prepare herself for bed when she receives a text from Beck requesting her presence downstairs. Ellie checks the time. She's not a night person, so starting a conversation at nine at night is something out of the ordinary for her. She declines with a text.

Marshall Beck is relentless. Ellie finally concedes and meets him in the lounge. He drinks a beer, but it's not his first of the night while she sips on ginger ale. They discuss their lives over the last ten years. Beck admits to Ellie he should never have let her go. He should have been strong enough to make it work. Beck reaches out to touch Ellie's hand when she pulls it back. He makes eye contact and tells her he wants a shot with her one more time. She explains her relationship with Digger, but Beck pushes forward, stating he didn't realize how much he loved her until he saw her again.

Without a reply to Beck's statement, Ellie searches for a way out of the lounge. "Marshall, I shouldn't have met you. We had our chance a long time ago. I must leave." Ellie places her arm on the table to slide from the booth, but when she does, Beck places his hand on Ellie's arm.

Just as Beck touches Ellie, Watson walks up to the booth. "Need any help, Ellie?"

Chapter 7

"No, Watson, she doesn't need help. We're just having a private conversation." Beck fumes as he glares at Watson.

Ellie turns to Watson, and Beck still has her arm. She grimaces from Beck's pressure. When her eyes widen, Watson steps up to Beck. "Release her arm, now." Watson's face turns a vivid red as the veins pop out in his neck.

Beck throws Ellie's arm in the air as he releases it and exclaims, "better, now?" Beck slides out of the booth and stands face to face with Watson. Neither one backing down.

Watson, taking the high road, says, "have a good evening, Beck."

With the exchange over, Watson glances at Ellie, "what were you thinking meeting him alone? Does Digger know you are down here?"

Ellie stammers with her head down, "Beck insisted we meet to catch up. Nothing else. Obviously, he had other intentions. Digger doesn't know I'm with Beck. I'll tell him, though, because this secret is not one I can keep. I fear Beck will cause problems for us, anyway."

Watson doesn't comment on Beck because he's deciding on Beck's future with the team. Larkin just might be the lead detective by morning. "Come on. I'll walk you to your room."

The duo exits the lounge, and on the way to the door, Beck makes a snide comment. "Ignore him, Watson. He's had too much to drink. He might not remember tonight if he keeps drinking." Ellie suggests.

As Ellie and Watson step off the elevator, Digger stands at his door, looking up and down the hallway. "There you are. What happened? You two swallow a canary or something."

Watson graciously bows out of the meeting and leaves Ellie with Digger. Ellie walks into the room and leans out the door, and says, "Thanks, Watson."

With a half wave over his shoulder, Watson heads back to the elevators for a ride up to the next floor. He's furious with Ellie for meeting Beck alone, and he's mad at Beck for inviting her. Should he remove Beck from the task force? Can Ellie and Beck get past this argument?

Ellie shares her experience with Digger. She describes the entire meeting with Beck and how his mood went from melancholy to violent within an hour. When Beck grabbed her arm, Watson walked up to their table. Ellie admits she was lucky with Watson's appearance. If Watson were not there, she would have involved the bartender. Ellie doesn't remember Beck having a temper or a drinking problem, but maybe the years have changed him. Taking Digger's hands in hers, Ellie asks Digger for forgiveness.

Digger leans in and kisses Ellie, accepting her apology. They retire to their rooms for the night, eager to begin fresh tomorrow. But Digger has trouble letting the incident go.

Larkin joins the group for breakfast. He notices the lack of sleep on Ellie's face. With politeness to his tone, he asks, "Are you okay, Ellie?"

"I'm fine, Larkin. Not much sleep, and when I did rest, it was restless. After coffee and food, I'll be ready." Ellie explains.

No one bothers to ask Digger about his lack of sleep. He slept little last night too. The scene Ellie described between her and Beck replayed in his head all night. How can a man treat a woman like that? Better yet, did he and Ellie have a stable relationship back in the day or a casual thing?

As breakfast ends, Larkin's cell phone rings with a call from the medical examiner. He steps away from the table to take the call. The medical examiner explains they located a Pittsburg doctor who treated Mr. and Mrs. Teeter. The doctor wondered where the Teeter's went when they stopped seeing him. Both were in good health for their age. The medical doctor gave us the most significant find- the Teeter's dentist. The identification came using dental records for Gerald and Opal Teeter and the reminder the second set of bones remains unidentified.

Larkin rejoins the group with a smile on his face. He shares the news, and everyone claps. Digger's concentration moves now to the second set of bones. He doesn't rest until he exhausts all avenues.

All skeletons are identifiable, and he must follow the path until he knows all information.

The team climbs into Larkin's vehicle for the ride into town. They work on the case files again. Larkin's gut tells him the crimes connect through the public defender's office, but he's unsure how yet. Since the parole officer lists didn't pan out, there is no other option left to investigate.

Just as the ignition turns off, Watson receives a call from Beck. Someone discovered another murder in downtown Pittsburgh less than an hour ago. Watson asks Beck for the address and advises the team is on their way.

This victim is Asian, and he lives in an upstairs apartment above a restaurant. The restaurant owner found the victim when he failed to show for work. The victim sustained a fatal injury four days ago if we go by the restaurant owner's timeline.

Ellie steps into the apartment first, and the smell hits her like a freight train. If she had known about this murder, she would have skipped breakfast. Once steady, she proceeds into the kitchen area and spots the victim gagged and tied to a kitchen table chair. His head droops at an odd angle too. This is the first scene she noticed the dried blood spatter and the clotted blood drops on the victim. Ellie spots the shooter's location and the same elongated blood drops as before. The killer must have worn the same shoes and or pants to create the identical pattern.

Digger walks up behind Ellie, and he whispers in her ear, "Beck is outside. I'll walk with you."

A nod of Ellie's head suggests she received the message. She continues her survey of the apartment. Then her attention turns to the victim's chest, and there is a diagonal straight line from the middle of the chest outward towards the hip bone. These markings are strange. If this killer takes one mark for each victim, he could kill for a while, depending on the picture. Now, she has another one for her note cards.

Nothing of added interest shows itself in the survey. Digger advises Ellie that Larkin and Watson will speak with the owner about the victim. They rely on information about his past from the restaurant owner, who seems close to the victim.

After the apartment inspection, the duo heads downstairs to join the conversation with the restaurant owner. The older man has unshed tears in his eyes as he speaks of the victim. He shares how the victim was turning his life around by staying away from gangs. The young Asian was a fantastic cook and served the daily lunch crowd. Ellie interjects a question for the owner, "does your restaurant serve the same people during the lunch hour?"

Digger understood the question and smiled at Ellie for thinking of it. Then, digger expounded on it because of the language issue, "do you recall the same person eating lunch and talking with the victim?"

In his hard-to-understand accent, the owner describes several people who eat lunch at the restaurant multiple times a week. Larkin and Ellie jot the descriptions down in their books as the older man spoke.

With the victim being in and out of prison several times, Larkin inquired if any of the victim's cellmates kept in touch with him. The owner shook his head vigorously. "I permit no one from the prison to visit the apartment. However, if they've eaten lunch at the restaurant, I'm unaware."

Watson finishes the questions by asking the owner if he knows the names of the folks he described. He shakes his head again because he has no names, just faces. Watson suspected that, but he needed confirmation.

Since they inspected the apartment and the restaurant owner questioned, the team piles into Larkin's vehicle to ride to police headquarters. Ellie sketches the descriptions of the patrons in her book. So far, none appear familiar.

Ellie continues sketching, and when finished, two faces look vaguely familiar, but who knows from where. She asks Larkin to verify the likeness from the owner's description. He changes one sketch and then agrees. They make copies of each sketch for the group. It would be nice to have a name to go with the faces.

When the team sits at the table, Larkin shares the sketches and asks if anyone recognizes a face. Several admit they appear familiar but nothing concrete. One officer asks for Beck, but no one knows his whereabouts. The officer then directs his question to Larkin, "do you want us to show these around the scenes and see if anyone recognizes them?"

Larkin jumps on the idea. "Another superb idea. Split up with your same teams and revisit your scenes. Report back tomorrow at lunch unless you hear something today."

Watkins entered the room as the officers filed out. "What's the rush?"

Larkin shares the plan with Watson while waving the sketches, then he asks, "Where is Beck? Shouldn't he be here for the meeting?"

"He should be here. Beck didn't tell me if he had another stop after the crime scene. His communication skills are lacking. I'll speak to him today." Watson states with an air of determination. This case is sticky with the past relationship with Beck and Ellie, but Beck's behavior is peculiar.

Bob joins the team in the conference room and picks up a file. He reviews the notes on the boards. If the team has ruled out cellmates, prisons, arresting officers, and parole officers, the only idea is an attorney. "Hey, quick question, has anyone ruled out the victim's attorneys? From the looks of this list, the attorney isn't listed."

Digger, Ellie, and Larkin stand from their chair and walk to the boards. "No, we haven't ruled them out, Bob, because no one mentioned attorneys. So grab the files, and we'll check out the attorneys now." Digger prompted.

After they log every case file, Bob reads the board. "Public defender is the key. The public defender's office represented all victims. Now, we need to go back through the files and find the name of the public defender to see if one person represented the victims."

"Bob, you might be onto something here. This is promising." Larkin gives Bob a fist bump as he pulls the first file from the stack and reads off the first name, Silas Hanson.

They added tick marks and names to the board with each file. Silas Hanson represented five of our victims, while Tara Jiffs represented two, along with Oscar Gomez. With there being three public defenders mentioned, the killer is not after one specific person. Ellie considers the information, "is the killer after the public defender's office, or did the killer spend time in jail with these victims? Is that how they knew each other?"

"It makes sense if they were in the system together. But, if none of the victims were cellmates with each other, we need to run the cellmate list by the list of public defenders and see if a name pops." Digger points out.

One case file after another opens, and we add the victim's cellmate to the board. Two files are missing cellmate information. Larkin calls for the information, and while we wait for a return call, we discuss scenarios.

After several minutes of brainstorming, Larkin produces the final two cellmates. Another disheartening discovery, no matches. The group shares empty stares. "Okay, guys, so it's not the cellmates. The public defender's office is still a viable possibility." Watson points out to his teammates.

Larkin places his palms into his eyes and rubs. The group is frustrated. "My suggestion is to invite the three public defenders into the office in the morning. We'll have a round table discussion on their knowledge of the victims. Thoughts?"

"Do it, Larkin. Make the call now. I'd like to know we have something to work with in the morning instead of having no direction. Your officer teams should have some information tomorrow too." Watson stands and walks to the back table for his endless supply of coffee.

An hour later, we set the meeting for nine in the morning. The public defenders agree to meet in police headquarters and will bring their victims' files. Unfortunately, Silas nor Tara realized the number of murders amongst their group. Oscar questioned the murders to his superior, but no one acted upon the information.

Since the team has a morning meeting, they decide to break for the day. Everyone's brain is tired, trying to process the information. From the carvings to the cellmates to the public defender's office, the connection is there. The group doesn't notice it yet.

As night fell, Ellie enjoyed downtime with a book. Just as she dozes off, her cell phone signals a text message. Startled, her book falls to the floor at the same time her cell phone does. She plucks her phone and book from the floor and glances at her phone. Beck's name is on the lock screen. Her messages open, and he's asking for a repeat performance tonight. With her answer in the reply box, she sends it. Thinking the conversation over, she turns out the light and lays down for the night.

Fifteen minutes later, another text message from Beck. He begs to meet because he wants to apologize in person. Ellie replies with a message advising Beck she accepts his apology but does not want to meet. She expresses her tiredness.

Beck continues texting Ellie, and Ellie stops replying. Then Beck calls her cell phone, leaving messages. By midnight, Ellie is nervous. If Beck is downstairs in the bar, would he come to her room? He can't enter without a key, right? Beck's actions scare her, so she taps on Digger's door again.

"I'm so sorry to wake you, but I have a situation. Here." Ellie hands her phone to Digger, and he loses his cool.

"What is wrong with this guy? Is he here in the bar?" Digger fumes.

"He never says in his text or voice messages, but he won't stop. He isn't welcome in my room. Digger, how can I stop this guy? I'm ready to go home and forget about Pittsburgh. The locals can track this killer. They have enough information from us to find him. Will you go home with me?"

"I'll go home with you. However, I've never known you to back down from anything." Digger studies her face.

"Things changed for me after the stabbing. I'm more afraid of confrontation than ever before. Beck is an alcoholic, and he needs help, but I'm not the one to provide it." Ellie explains.

Digger runs his hands through his hair as he paces. "Let me speak with Watson. He needs to know we are leaving and why. He'll be furious, but he can manage with Larkin and Bob."

With the phone to his ear, Digger calls Watson and explains the situation. Watson wants to meet them, and they agree to meet in Digger's room. While the pair wait for Watson, another text message arrives. Beck admits to being in the lounge waiting for her. A knock sounds from Digger's door, and he opens it for Watson.

Watson's face is bright red with rage. "Where is this guy? It's time I end this craziness."

"Here's Ellie's phone. Read the messages for yourself. He gets more aggressive as the night matures. Beck has a drinking issue, Watson. He doesn't act like this during the day. It's only after a few drinks, and then the aggression shows its ugly face."

"I'm going downstairs and have a word with him." Watson walks to the door as Digger calls out.

"Wait, Watson. You can't go alone. If he gets violent, you need a witness and help. Let me put on my shoes, and I'll go with you. Ellie, stay in your room. Do not open it for anyone but us. Keep the bar across the door." Digger pecks Ellie on the cheek and exits with Watson.

Ellie paces as she waits for word on the encounter between the men. She can't believe it has come to this. Beck has never acted this way before. Is it alcohol or another drug? The stars shine bright as Ellie stares out the window praying for safety for her men.

Watson enters the lounge first with Digger on his heels. Beck sits in a booth in the back. His head is down, and his hair is messy. Watson slides in the booth on the opposite side, then Digger follows. "What is wrong with you, Beck? We saw the messages you sent to Ellie. You're frightening her."

Beck pauses before he answers, "I didn't mean to scare her. I only want to talk. You prevented our talk the other night."

"I stopped it because you wouldn't let her leave. Are you an alcoholic, Beck? If so, you need help. As of now, you are no longer a task force member. Detective Larkin is your replacement. I'll meet with your superior tomorrow morning to file a complaint."

Beck's mouth hangs open in astonishment. "Why are you treating me this way? You can't control me after hours. I'm a good detective."

Digger raises his hand as if to diffuse the situation. "Beck, listen, no one has said anything about your ability as a detective. But, when you drink, you get volatile, and that's no good for anyone. Ellie doesn't want to meet you now or in the future. She has asked me to take her home now because she wants to forget Pittsburgh. Remove her phone number from your phone and never contact her again."

Watson adds, "Beck, you need help with the drinking. Don't throw your career away because of a bottle. It's not worth it."

Beck nods his agreement and slides out of the booth without uttering another word. After watching him leave, Watson and Digger retreat to Digger's room, where Ellie is frantic.

A knock comes from her door, but it roots her feet to the floor. Another knock, then she walks over to the door and hears Digger and Watson discussing the situation. Ellie opens the door, and both men smile back. They enter the room and rehash the conversation with Beck. Both men assure her, Beck will not cause her any more anxiety.

After the men depart her room, Ellie ponders the night's events. Did she exaggerate Becks' emotions? No, she did not, as Digger witnessed the text messages on her phone. Why does she feel so bad for Beck? She doesn't want him to ruin his career over an altercation with her. There must be a way for her to help him. Ellie falls into a restless sleep filled with dreams of Digger and Beck.

Chapter 8

Morning came in a rush for Ellie, and the foursome devoured breakfast together. Ellie has trouble making eye contact with the guys. She feels horrible about last night, and she's not sure how to approach the subject. Sipping coffee gives her hands and mind something to do.

A few minutes pass when Watson advises the group that Larkin is aware of last night's encounter with Beck. Ellie slowly brings her eyes to meet his. His face shows nothing but empathy. Still, Ellie is uncomfortable discussing this situation. The feeling will not leave her alone. For Ellie, this is too emotional.

Digger takes Ellie's hand, "that wasn't your fault. Beck is unstable."

"I might not have made him that way, but I sure helped him along the way. I should never have met him, but I couldn't stop myself. We've known each other for a long time, and nothing like this entered my mind." Ellie explains as she bows her head.

Then it's Larkin's turn to help improve her attitude, "Ellie, things happen in people's lives, things no one can control. Beck might have had something in his past that still rears its ugly head occasionally. You can't go on thinking this is your fault. We all have to make choices and live with the results."

Ellie lifts her head and looks at each man sitting at her table. "You guys are the best. Thank you all for being here with me. I apologize for bringing drama to your task force. If I thought Beck would have done this, I would have stayed away."

Watson clears the air, and things appear settled. The foursome drive to police headquarters. Ellie watches the city pass her window while trying to come to terms with Beck. One day she hopes to be rid of the uneasiness.

When the group arrives at police headquarters, Bob stands by the conference room door. "I wondered if you remembered the meeting this morning. Nothing like being right on time." Bob turns and enters the room with the group following.

Silas Hanson, Tara Jiffs, and Oscar Gomez, public defenders, sit at one end of the table. Other members of the task force take their seats while Ellie and Digger sit side by side. Digger keeps a watch on Ellie as he knows she is not okay with Beck's situation.

Watson begins the meeting by expressing his gratitude for the public defender's willingness to help the task force capture a killer. Next, he introduces the three visitors. The task force wants any information on the victims which could lead them to the killer. Watson emphasizes the murderer kills his victims with a small-caliber handgun and then carves a picture or a symbol into the victim's chest area.

Tara Jiffs, the young public defender, apparently has experienced nothing like Watson's crime description. A few of the task force members watch Tara's face pale and her hands tremble. Watson offers visual photos to help the public defenders, but they decline the offer.

With the files separated on the table, Larkin takes over the meeting. "Each of you represented multiple victims. Please share what you know about the victims with us. The task force will gather information on each victim to find a commonality, which will lead us to the killer."

Silas raises his hand and offers to go first. Larkin passes Silas's files to him and gives him a few moments to review them. "I had all these cases. Are you sure five victims are mine?"

Watson answers with a swift, "yes, Silas, you had five, Tara has two, and Oscar has two as of now."

Silas remembered a few because he only scanned them, but the older ones, he had to read the file to refresh his memory. Silas has been a public defender for forty years and counting. He is older, ragged, and a bit tired. Tara, on the other hand, is Silas's opposite. She is a petite girl in her mid-twenties with only two years under her belt. In the middle is Oscar. He is middle-aged who transferred to Pennsylvania from Ohio for unknown personal reasons.

None of the public defenders realized they had multiple murdered offenders. They all claim workload diverted their attention from the deaths. If offenders stay out of trouble, they have no reason to check in on them until their trial hits the docket. Once on the docket, they meet with the assigned offenders regularly. Until then, they leave that to the parole officer.

Digger jots a note to speak with the parole officer for each victim. The task force didn't consider the parole officer's side since no victims had the same parole officer. They might help with the investigation.

Silas announces his readiness to begin. The first one was in the city. He represented an Asian guy who the police arrested for theft, burglary with a weapon. This was his second arrest. Silas admits he closed the file and moved on to the next one when they notified him of the offender's death.

The second case involves Jeffrey Cooke. Silas thought Jeffrey might turn his life around while at the halfway house. He was a good kid that got caught with drugs and alcohol distribution to a minor. The charges were not substantial, and Jeffrey didn't have a prior record. He was dead before his trial hit the docket.

Again, Silas spoke of a young Spanish guy who he thought could turn things around. This offender had issues with DUI and drug possession for the third time. He likely would have been sentenced to prison, but he wouldn't have stayed longer. Silas figured a rival gang member killed this kid.

Corbin Matthews is the victim in the following case. "This guy was mean. He had the darkest eyes of anyone I've ever seen. There would have been no way to rehabilitate this guy. The police busted him for carjacking with a weapon, but his record is lengthy. It didn't surprise me to hear of his demise."

Last, Silas finishes his list with a black guy who did jail time for drug distribution. The offender pled guilty and gave up his supplier for a lighter sentence. He spent two years behind bars before his release and busted again for drugs within two weeks. He died four weeks before trial.

After Silas lays the last file down, he looks up at the crowd, "I didn't realize how many of my offenders have passed. It's a shame the city couldn't provide adequate help for young people who want it."

Silas passes the torch to Oscar, who clears his throat before beginning. The first case is a young black male who was a gang member. His arrest record ranges from theft, burglary, to robbery. Oscar shares this guy might have been okay if the gangs had left him alone.

Oscar's second case puzzled him when he heard of the death. This offender was an Asian guy who cooked at an eatery. While at a halfway house, he picked up the trade and learned from people there. The manager put the offender in touch with the restaurant owner. He was not a gang member, but he got arrested for burglarizing liquor stores. Oscar felt this guy could have turned his life around, too, if given a chance. The trial was two weeks away.

Tara finishes up the files on the table. "Detective Chavez notified me of the death. I never had time to meet either of these offenders. They were both killed shortly after my assignment. I believe

Detective Campagno handled this last one. I'm sorry I can't be of more help, but as I said, I never met them."

Watson stands and asks the task force if they have questions. He looks around the room as the members study their notes. When no one came forward, Watson mentions police protection for the public defenders. Silas declines. Tara stammers and then says she will think about it. Oscar waves it off too. Watson explains the killer is out for the people they represent. He nor the task force can guarantee their safety if the killer changes direction and goes after them.

As the three visitors stand to leave, Watson hands each a business card with explicit instructions to call his cell phone if anything seems out of the ordinary. They nod as they hurry to exit.

Once the visitors left, Watson asked the task force to remain in their seats. "I have something important to share with you. Beck is no longer the lead detective on the case. Detective Larkin assumes the lead. Don't bother asking questions about Beck. It was best for the task force. Does anyone have anything to share?"

One teammate raises his hand, "we have nothing new on the sketch. A kid riding a bicycle admits to seeing the guy in the sketch walking on the sidewalk by the apartment building where the murdered guy lived. The kid didn't know about the murder, and he ignored where the guy went. He said the guy kept his head down.

Digger addresses the task force, "we received the same information from another neighbor. From our meeting with the public defenders, I plan on contacting James Henderson. He is the parole officer for two of our victims. I need brushing up on how parole works."

The task force breaks for lunch. A young police officer from the task force walks over to Larkin and Digger. "I have a question about the public defenders and their cases. How long have the public defenders had their cases before their death?"

Larkin glances at Digger, and then Digger studies the board. "Interesting question, Officer Rafter. You wonder if we can work the case in reverse."

"Why not, sir? If we can get an idea of how long each victim survived before a public defender assignment, then we might get lucky. The killer knows these people are awaiting trial. I'm not sure how, but he knows."

With head bobs, Larkin and Digger think about the suggestion. "I like it. Officer Rafter, would you help review the files for dates and such? We can make a list from there."

"It would delight me to help." Officer Rafter expresses as he nods his head.

"Let's eat lunch. Then we can start on the new list. I like that idea more and more, Rafter." Larkin pats Rafter on the back as the group heads for the car. Watson places a call to Rafter's commander advising he is working the task force today and would not be on patrol.

Lunch takes place at a diner within walking distance of police headquarters. The diner has been in business for decades, and it sits partially under an expressway overpass. No one expected the diner to continue in business when the overpass came to town. But the locals couldn't watch it leave. The business thrives, and lunchtime is the favorite.

Luckily for the group, the owners love when law enforcement stops in for a bite. The group accepts a round table in the back. It afforded not much privacy, but the gesture was nice. Service was impeccable, as always.

On the walk back, Watson answers a phone call. His face turns shades of red. "You are kidding me? How did that happen, and better yet, how did they find out? I'm walking into headquarters now. Set them up outside on the steps. Maybe sweating a little will change their mind." With an enormous sigh, Watson slides his phone into his pants pocket.

"I'm pushing our afternoon meeting back an hour. Police headquarters called. There are a media presence waiting for the task force because they want a statement about 'The Carver'. Precisely, they are yelling about being kept in the dark." Watson exclaims.

The group shakes their heads in astonishment. "No one is hiding the murders. We've just decided not to share them yet. We're trying to gather more information." Ellie adds.

Watson is furious, and no one can blame him. Someone notified the media, and Ellie knows who that someone might be. Ellie leans into Digger, "do you think Beck is capable of something like this?"

"Ellie, I do. Watson probably feels the same way. He just hasn't voiced it yet."

The conference room buzzes with the news of the media hanging around. Officer Rafter takes a seat in front of the file stack. He works on the list by himself while others tend to the media.

Bob steps in to help Watson write his press releases. Bob is such a natural writer because of his word choices. He can mold anything to say whatever you want. Fifteen minutes later, Watson has his press release. It will take about ten minutes to deliver. Then he must answer questions. Digger will help with the problems and for crowd control.

The day is sunny with no breeze, and the steps and the curb are full of media persons and their TV crew. So it surprised Watson when he opened the door, and he saw the multitude of people waiting for his remarks.

The media quieten as Watson and his entourage walk to the bank of microphones. His press release begins by thanking the media for their attendance. The statement gives them only minimal information about the murders, and then he moves onto the task force. No one interrupts him during his speech, but when the speech ends, chaos ensues.

One TV lady, Watson recognizes, raises her hand, and yells, "Why hasn't the FBI captured 'The Carver' yet? This killer has been active for a long time. Does Pennsylvania need a new FBI Special Agent to take over?"

Watson takes a deep breath and replies. "The task force continues to gather information and follow up on each lead. We will get this guy."

Again, the same TV reporter, "Have you determined the picture the killer is drawing?"

Digger walks over to the microphone, "We don't yet, but we are closer. The task force has leads to work. We'll share when additional information is available." Digger leans over to Watson and tells him to answer his phone.

Watson answers, "it's Ellie. Beck is in the media group on the left side in the back. He looks rough. We just wanted you to know, and this is a quick way to end the press conference."

While he speaks with Ellie, Watson enters police headquarters and takes a deep breath. "The press conference was horrible. That TV reporter, I want to know her name. We may have to contact her directly and have her cool her heels."

Larkin adds, "her name is Kelly Knight. Everyone calls her KK. She's been a long-time Pittsburgh resident. Kelly doesn't like Pittsburgh police too much. Someone mugged her while she walked in the park, and the mugger remained on the loose.

She blames us. Kelly always tries to diminish our work."

"Do you think she will divulge the anonymous tip?" Ellie asks Larkin.

"No way. She is all constitutional. She spent time in jail because she refused to give up her informants. Kelly is a seasoned reporter. I would say some people are a little scared of her. She knows everyone in the right circle."

Watson nods in agreement. "One of those kind bothers me nosing around here. It makes me wonder what information she currently holds and if she shares the wrong information with the public. Suppose I should try to meet with her and keep her on my side."

Bob suggests giving it a day or two and watch her newscast in the meantime. After we see one or two, she'll give away what she knows. Then, we can change how we communicate with the press. We keep Kelly Knight close to us. We might need her to help find a killer. It would be nice to have her on our side.

Chapter 9

With the press release over, Watson calls it a day. It upsets him someone leaked the information and with himself for not preparing sooner. The media always finds out about murders. The task force has been lucky so far not to hear from the press until today. Why today? Did Beck call Kelly Knight? They probably know each other. Beck's career has spanned decades, and so has Kelly's, both in the same town.

Watson advises the task force he's calling off for the rest of the day. If they have additional work to handle, then get it done. Report to the conference room at eight in the morning. Watson tells Bob he's catching a cab to the hotel and asks him to stay with Digger and Ellie.

Upon entering the conference room, Digger and Ellie expected to see Watson, but Bob told them he was on his way to the hotel. Bob explains Watson needs a little alone time. He needs to think through a few issues.

Officer Rafter invites the task force to sit. He shares, "all the victims received their public defender assignment from two weeks to three months before their murder. Is it possible to see the public defender's case files where the offenders were assigned for up to three months? I'm not sure how many people that will be, but we need to know the number."

Ellie asks, "Is there anything else in your numbers that could lower our count? Such as the age of the victim or the victim's address."

A pause before he replies, "I didn't look at those details, but it would help to know. I'll go back through the file and jot that information."

Digger slips into a chair and slides it under the table. "Pass me a file, and I'll help. This might give us the answers we need to find this guy."

Suppertime comes and goes as the group works to finish the list. Bob provides sub sandwiches for everyone while they work. As the sun slides downward, the task force leans back in its chairs and stretches.

Officer Rafter tabulates the list and seems satisfied with the results. "Interesting information. Our victim's range in age from high teens to low twenties, all arrested before, crimes were not major with the only question being the home invasion, and they all live alone in neglected areas of town. With that much detail, our public defender's list should narrow considerably. Your thoughts?"

Everyone studies the information presented. Larkin raises his head, "I'm submitting a request to the public defender's office for a list of offenders with these criteria. Office Rafter, thank you for your idea. You've been instrumental to the team."

"Thanks, Detective Larkin. I'm glad to be a part of it. Now, let's see if we can catch us a killer."

Larkin makes the call and discusses his parameters for the list. He hopes for a quick response as this list could prove fruitful for the team. While they wait, Larkin and Digger discuss the bones. "Digger, there are no recent revelations on the remaining bones. Until we have some idea who they are, we can't ID them."

"What about having the skulls sent to a reconstructionist? They would give us an idea of their appearance. Once we have photos of the reconstructed skulls, we can ask the neighbor we located or even ask Kelly Knight for help. She can showcase the skulls on air. Maybe someone would recognize the pair." Digger suggests.

"I don't know the first thing about working with a reconstructionist. That's out of my element. Would you have a contact, Digger?"

"Yes. I can call the lady we used for the melee in Montana. She's on the east coast, so shipping the skulls from here wouldn't be as cumbersome for us as Montana. I'll make the call now. Cross your fingers that she has a spot for us." Digger stood from his chair and walked to the window. While on the phone, Digger watches as Beck walks around the parking lot. Beck seems to look for a vehicle as he stops at every black Suburban and peers through the window. Digger waves Larkin and Bob to the window. Ellie follows, too, because she wants to witness the excitement as well. The group watches Beck as he continues his trek through the parking lot.

Digger steps away from the window to notate the reconstructionist's shipping address. They speak a little longer before the call ends. "The reconstructionist is available for us. We'll need to ship the skulls tomorrow, if possible, no later than the day after. Can you call the medical examiner? I'll package the bones for shipping when we get the clearance."

Back to the window, "Did Beck do anything on his walk?"

Ellie answers, "Not a thing but walked around and peeked into car windows. He's acting so strangely. What could he be searching for? Has he lost his car?"

Officer Rafter speaks from the back of the group, "Detective Beck drives a dark brown Crown Vic and has for years."

The group turns and faces Officer Rafter, and he shrugs his shoulders. "Beck has been acting differently for a while now. No one knows what's wrong with him. He refuses to discuss it."

Beck leaves the parking lot in his dark brown Crown Vic and squeals his tires as he makes his turn. Shortly after, they hear sirens traveling away from headquarters. Larkin glances at Rafter, "can you go to dispatch and see if Beck received a response call? Just for curiosity's sake."

The group watches Rafter leave the office. Larkin looks at each task force member. "What I'm about to say does not leave this room. Check your vehicles for explosives before driving from the lot. Beck has a background in explosives, and he just might be angry enough to cause damage. Be on alert. Travel in pairs. Our day is over. We'll work on the list tomorrow morning."

Bob drives Digger and Ellie to the hotel after a visual check on the vehicle. "Feels like old times, doesn't it?"

"Thanks for the reminder, Bob. I just pray we all make it out of this one unscathed." Ellie states as vivid memories come rushing back.

The trio separates as they reach their rooms. Today was long, but they felt it was productive. There is an air of excitement around Officer Rafter's list. Ellie refreshes her mind with the carvings by shifting the cards and studying the picture. Nothing comes to mind. It's nothing but lines and two curly ques. Ellie notices they didn't receive a new murder today. Based on the killer's prior timetable, today would have marked another death. Wonder what changed for the killer? Is there an undiscovered murder?

Digger sits on his bed and studies the carvings, just as Ellie does. The carvings confuse him too. He lays his cards out like a puzzle and moves the pieces around, hoping a picture materializes. Digger gives up and tries to sleep. He works through the bones and how they might relate to this murder. The bone discovery is too coincidental to the murders. Nothing good happens when you find bones and have a serial killer in the same area.

The sun rose bright, and the group met in the hotel dining room. Larkin ambles over to the group, so they drag a chair over to the table. "I have the list, and I'll admit it is promising. I've asked Officer Rafter to join us this morning. The biggest surprise was the number of people assigned to the public defender's office. How about over two thousand? I never knew there was such a large number."

Digger chokes on his coffee. "We can't possibly investigate that many people. I guessed around a hundred for our little group, but I was way off."

Larkin chuckles, "Digger, the number I repeated is the total number of offenders, not for our group. The list we ordered shows us, ninety-seven people. Nine of which turn four months at the public defender's office in two days. Our list is doable. We'll split it and see where it goes. I've requested the files for the remaining eighty-eight."

The group takes a collective sigh of relief. Everyone's mood is buoyant when they hear the number. Ellie speaks up, "Has anyone spoken to Watson? He usually makes it downstairs for breakfast."

Bob raises his head. "He's already at the office. Watson met with Detective Beck's superior this morning."

"Uh, how did it go? Or should I ask?" Ellie inquires while rubbing her hands together.

"I haven't heard yet, but we'll see Watson soon since the task force is meeting."

The group finishes breakfast and meets at the vehicle for the ride to the police headquarters. Ellie fidgets on the car ride, and Digger leans over to console her. She peeks up into Digger's eyes, trying to speak, but nothing comes out. Digger rubs her arm as a measure of reassurance. She leans her head back on the seat, wondering if Beck will take out his frustration on her.

Watson waits for his team at the conference room edge. "Good morning. I'm sure Bob explained about my early morning meeting. I spoke with Beck's superior, and they mentioned Beck has been acting strange too. Several people have mentioned it, but no one has filed a complaint. They're meeting with him this morning too."

Ellie asks, "does anyone know what changed? Why the personality change?"

"I didn't ask, Ellie. He isn't my agent, so I left it up to his superiors." Watson responds.

Ellie nods her head in understanding, but the curiosity remains. Why has Beck changed? People don't change unless something provokes like alcohol or a person or both. Ellie tells herself to let it go. Beck is not her concern.

Larkin stands in the room's front, ready to start the meeting. He waits as Ellie, Digger, and Watson find a chair. "The numbers are in," he begins. "We have eighty-eight files to work through this morning. Thanks to Officer Rafter for his idea, we're working with offenders assigned to a public defender within the last three months. We whittled the number down with nine exceeding the three months in two days. So, eighty-eight it is."

Eyes shift around the room. Happy to have a lower number, but the task at hand is nothing short of monumental. Each twosome will take eight files and fill out a questionnaire. Larkin continues, "It's a list of items we need from each file. I requested an audit per our requirements, but they couldn't run it. So, we are going old school with paper and pen."

Ellie and Digger pluck the top eight from the stack and begin their research. It's time-consuming searching for the information they need, but each member feels this will help find the killer. Digger scratches his head and states, "the killer hasn't shown up in the last few days."

"I thought about the killer last night. It is strange. Wonder what made him stop?" Ellie questions.

"Anything, I guess. If he had watched television, Kelly's story might have scared him, and he gave up. Or he might wait for the next available time to strike. It would be nice to capture him before he kills again."

"Amen, Digger," Watson interjects. "Speaking of Kelly, she requests another press conference today. I advised her we were in task force meetings today, working through new information, and tomorrow would be the earliest I could have another conference."

"How did she take being put off, Watson?" Ellie asks.

"Not too well. She claims we are hiding information from the press, which I told her we are not."

"Invite her up here, Watson. Show her we are working through files. I know we can't tell her about the files specifically, but maybe a visual will help her. Then play to her good side. Tell her we'll come to her first as soon as something breaks." Bob suggests.

All eyes are on Bob when Larkin breaks the silence, "I like it, Bob. If Kelly knows she's getting first dibs on something, she might play ball with us. Watson, why don't you and Bob take her to lunch? Someplace quiet, you can talk."

Bob and Watson glance at each other when Watson replies, "Make the plans, Bob. It's your show."

Bob steps away from the group and places a call to Kelly. The group hears him talking and then the wait. Kelly comes back on the line agreeing to lunch.

"Lunch plans accepted. Time is approaching. Finish up, Watson, and we'll be on our way. Kelly is very receptive to working with us. She's never worked closely with the FBI before." Bob shares with his eyebrows lifted and a grin.

Office Rafter stands and clears his throat. Eyes and heads shift his way. "When you complete your paperwork, if you can turn them into me, I'm gathering the data." Papers slide down the table toward Rafter. He grabs them before they skitter to the ground. "The results will be ready this afternoon. Maybe we can meet around one or two."

Larkin agrees with the timetable as his phone rings. "I'll tell him. Thanks, Doc."

"Digger, the medical examiner's office has space for you to package the skulls. He's waiting for you if you can make the time now. If not, I'll call him back to rearrange a time."

"Now is good for me, Larkin. Ellie, why don't you come along? You have experience with skulls."

Ellie and Digger exit the conference room after handing Rafter their last questionnaire. Larkin follows and walks them to the medical examiner's office. "This shouldn't be too long, Larkin. Ellie and I will come back to the conference room as soon as we finish." Larkin opens the medical examiner's office door with a nod of approval and lets the duo inside.

Over the next hour, the duo slides into a rhythm, packaging the skulls for shipping. Digger confirms with the reconstructionist the skull's arrival tomorrow. There is nothing more for Digger to do on the skulls but wait.

Digger signs for the shipment of skulls and turns to Ellie. "Thanks for helping with this. It went much quicker with two people."

"It's time for lunch, and then Rafter can share his results. This could be the answer we've been searching for, Digger. I'm ready to get home."

"I'm more ready for our talk than I am for home."
Digger plants a soft kiss on her cheek as they walk
to police headquarters. Digger takes his lanyard and
swipes the back door to headquarters. They've
made this trek so many times in the past they know
their way to the conference room.

When the elevator doors open, the task force greets
them. "Stay on. We are heading to lunch." Watson
advises and then reminds them he and Bob are
taking Kelly to lunch.

"No problem with us." Digger and Ellie scoot closer
together so the others can enter. The ride was quiet.
Then Digger asks, "anything happened while we
were away?"

Rafter looks at Digger over his shoulder and grins.
"Get ready to dig in when we get back from lunch.
Results are in. Don't ask. I'll share when we
return."

Everyone walks to the diner on the next block. As
they walk, Ellie feels like someone is staring at her.
She glances around but sees no one. The group
makes small talk about the weather and how ready
they are for summer to begin. The lunch crowd is
light as they enter. A large round table in the back is
open, and the group slides into the chairs. Just as
Ellie looks up, Beck is standing at the front window
staring at them. Ellie whispers to Digger to look at
the window.

Digger looks at the window and stands, then walks
to the front door. Larkin is right behind him. By the
time they reach the door, Beck is gone. They spot

him across the street on a bench waving at them. Larkin is furious. "Is this guy going to taunt us now? He is unstable. Let's eat and get back to headquarters. I'm ready to end this case."

When they reach the table, Ellie inquires, "did you speak with Beck?"

"No, we missed him. He waved at us from a bench across the street." Digger answers in a calm tone. He tries not to agitate Ellie. She feels uneasy about Beck being around, anyway. This episode will make things worse for her. Digger wants to put Ellie to work this afternoon by having her study Rafter's results. Since she notices patterns, she should spot one quickly.

The group reconvenes in the conference room after lunch. With full stomachs, staying awake proves difficult. Larkin orders full coffee urns delivered and stationed on the back wall of the conference room. "Coffee is ready. Grab a cup if you want before Rafter begins. This is important. Everyone needs to be on your A-game."

Rafter stands at the front of the table with papers in hand. His excitement is evident as he presents his findings to the group. Speaking to the group turns out to be easier than Rafter expected. The members are gracious and ask questions along the way. Rafter has each offender listed by race, age, address, the reason for arrest, public defender's assignment. He lays the papers on the table, and the group talks through ideas.

The list proves the offenders live in different areas. The courts assign the victims to one of the three public defenders already mentioned, which surprises Digger. Why only these three? There are a dozen or more public defenders available. Digger raises his hand and asks his question.

No one has an answer for him. So, he suggests pulling the offenders assigned to the three defenders, Silas, Oscar, and Tara.

With a separate stack in his hand, he waves it at Digger. "Already have them separated. I thought that might be a question. There are thirty-one of our eighty-eight assigned to our famous three. My suggestion is to start with this group and work out from there. Questions or ideas?"

Silence fills the room as the group studies the results of the report. Ellie lowers her head as she concentrates on the information. She flips pages in her notebook and makes marks with a purple highlighter. "I might have something. I'm not sure it means anything." Ellie stammers.

Larkin looks at her, "Well, tell us what you have."

"It's halfway housing. These victims spent time in a halfway house before moving to their current location." Ellie glances around the room as she waits for a reply.

Chapter 10

"How did you find this information, Ellie?" Larkin inquires with an eager tone.

"I've only checked our files, but all ten victims spent time in a halfway house. We need to look at the other files and see if they are a match. If so, we move on to the number of halfway houses involved." Ellie explains.

Rafter jumps up and looks at his list. "My files show halfway houses too."

Larkin's head spins with this information. "Do you think the killer stayed at a halfway house? Is this the connection we're searching for?"

"Could be, Larkin. But that would be a high number of potential people to investigate. I like the idea of using the files we have and cross-referencing those with the halfway houses." Digger suggests.

Larkin, as the lead detective, has the last word since Watkins is out. "Do it and do it now. We haven't had a murder for a few days. I can only imagine what's waiting for us somewhere. The killer is nowhere close to being through with his quest. Does anyone know the picture he is carving?"

Heads shake side to side around the room, giving Larkin the expected answer. The picture is still elusive. So far, it is a few lines on different areas of the victim's torso. What is the killer saying?

Larkin calls the public defender's office for a list of halfway houses closest to town, followed by the rest of the state. The office will email the file within the hour. While they wait, they discuss Watson and Kelly. All agree, making Kelly happy would be beneficial to the task force. A local TV personality might help reach the public quickly if they need it.

Twenty minutes later, Watson and Bob enter the room with Kelly following. Watson makes the introductions around the table. Kelly sits as if she's planning to stay. Digger and Ellie exchange glances as they're not sure what to talk about with a TV reporter in the room. Bob helps ease tension as he explains Kelly will help them get information to the public if needed, and she agrees not to browbeat Watson during the press conferences.

"Glad to have you on the team, Kelly." Rafter expresses.

"Thanks, Officer Rafter. I hear you helped the task force change direction on the investigation. I'd like to hear more about it when the time is right." Kelly states while looking at Watson.

"Sure thing, Kelly." Rafter lowers his head, not sure to continue the conversation.

Larkin's email alert sounds, and he grabs his laptop, eager to see the halfway houses list. Kelly senses her time to leave is now. Watson shows her the door and walks her out of the police headquarters. They chat more on the walk outside and realize they have a lot in common. Kelly suggests they have dinner together before he leaves Pittsburgh. Watson stammers but agrees. Not sure how to feel about the dinner, Watson pushes it from his brain. He has a case to settle.

As soon as Watson walks in the door without Kelly, Larkin shares the updates. It thrilled both Bob and Watson to hear of the halfway houses. "It makes perfect sense now that I've heard it. Is there a list of halfway houses in the area?"

"I have the list right here." Larkin waves the list above his head and continues, "There are forty-nine halfway houses in the state with twenty-one in the city and closest surrounding suburbs."

Watson suggests the same teams take two houses and ask questions of the offenders and survey the area. "If anyone seems questionable, get a name. Don't make appointments. Let's drop in on the halfway houses. The offenders might be at work. If so, find out where they work. Also, speak with the house manager, ask for their take on the offender.

The teams hit the streets with their recent assignments. Ellie, Digger, and Larkin take a mile drive to the halfway house closest to police headquarters. On entry, a middle-aged man asks if he can help them. Larkin steps forwards and produces his badge, then introduces Ellie and Digger. After explaining their visit, the man hands the group over to Chopper. Chopper runs this house and has for years. His home is for men only, eighteen years old and older, with strict rules. The group asks Chopper a lot of questions about the offenders on the list. Chopper provides answers but doesn't elaborate on anything. He's a man of brief words, but at least he answered the questions about the offenders. All the guys in the house must hold down a full-time job, or they can't stay. When the questions run out, the group retraces their steps to the door.

Digger and Larkin are in a hushed conversation as they walk toward the sidewalk. A younger guy passes the group, keeping his head down, never making eye contact. Ellie glances back over her shoulder and watches the young man enter the house. He carries bags of food in his arms. Wonder what role he plays at home? Chopper didn't mention any other workers.

With one more stop before the day ends, the group takes another halfway house downtown. This home doesn't compare to Chopper's. This one is nowhere as large, and the upkeep is less than favorable. It sits close to the train tracks, and the rumble of a passing train is loud. The trio enters the lobby to an empty desk. Ellie searches through the desk clutter for a service bell to ring but finds none.

Several minutes later, a young guy strolls into the room with a coke in hand. "Can I help you, folks?" He asked, startled.

Larkin steps up and explains their presence. The guy stutters as he tries to tell us, Larry, the manager, is out running an errand. The residents work during the day as the state mandates. Larkin leaves a note for Larry to call since the kid refused to release information on the residents. The kid states he has no authority to discuss the residents.

Digger checks his watch. He realizes he didn't hear from the reconstructionist. They agreed to text or email once she received the skeletons. He'll need to follow up. Also, he must remind her to make the skulls older.

Ellie asks Digger, "Everything okay, Digger?"

"I'm not sure. I haven't heard from the reconstructionist on the skull delivery. Usually, she texts me or emails. I have neither." Digger explains.

"She might be busy with another one. Give her time. She'll let you know." Ellie says to calm Digger.

Larkin gathers with Ellie and Digger at the vehicle. "Visiting these houses didn't help our investigation at all. Our offenders are still living at these houses."

"If you look at it like that, it didn't help. But consider we know the offenders at these two houses are safe. It's the houses with missing people that should give us concern." Ellie offers.

Digger and Larkin nod in agreement. "You're right, Ellie. We'll go back to headquarters and check-in with the others. Some teams won't report back until tomorrow because of distance to the houses."

Sitting at the conference room table, Watson watches television. "Are you looking for your reporter, Watson?" Digger asks as Bob snickers.

"She is not MY reporter, Digger. She is Pittsburgh's reporter. I wanted to see if she held up her end of the deal by lying low until we had something concrete."

Bob expresses his confidence in their understanding her focus will be on other topics.

Watson's face turns bright red, "What the?"

Bob states, "Watson, what has you in a twist?" Bob glances up and on the TV are their faces. All photos from different websites. Kelly used whatever photos she could find. Unfortunately, she found a lot of usable material from the Montana serial killer case.

"How could she do that after she agreed to lay back? I'm calling her." Bob is furious with himself and Kelly.

"No, don't call, Bob. I'm going to the station for a face-to-face. You can drive." Watson states. "Digger, Ellie, we'll drop you at the hotel on the way to the station."

"Let me pack my bag, and then I'm ready," Ellie said. Digger opts not to open his mouth. He is mad enough for everyone. How could she plaster their photos on the TV station? Wouldn't she think she could jeopardize the investigation? Now, the killer knows we're in town, and he knows what we look like. The killer has the upper hand with the new knowledge.

The car ride is silent as Watson stews in the front seat. "Sorry to have screwed up our task force. Kelly seemed genuine. We'll discuss it later."

Digger and Ellie exit the vehicle and walk into the lobby. The lobby clerk calls for Ellie, and she walks toward the counter. "Here is a note for you, Ms. Masters."

Ellie takes it and glances at Digger before opening it. She's apprehensive as she slides her finger under the flap. She takes out the paper and reads it. Unbelievable. This guy won't stop. "Beck wants me to call him Digger."

Digger takes the card, reads it, and slides it back into the envelope. "I'll call him for you and discuss it with him."

Ellie and Digger split at their rooms. Detective Beck is driving a wedge between them, and neither Ellie nor Digger know how to handle it. Once in his room, Digger takes a chair at the window and calls Beck. Beck doesn't answer, so Digger leaves a polite voicemail asking him to return the call.

Digger closes his eyes at midnight after he gives up on Beck returning his call. The realization hit when Digger concedes Beck might not return his call, ever. Another method of communication must prevail. Before sleep takes over, Digger sends a text message to Beck outlining the situation. Digger explains Ellie does not want contact with him, and he should refrain from contacting Ellie to thwart an ugly confrontation. Once delivered, Digger lays back on the bed and falls asleep. Except for the overnight dreams, when he awakes, Digger is ready to start the day.

After breakfast, on the drive to headquarters, Watson calls headquarters for an update. He wanted to prepare the group for their arrival. Watson's face turns crimson red as Larkin updates him on the situation downstairs.

"It seems we have an issue at headquarters. Since the media posted our pictures on the television, the other town reporters flocked to the front steps of police headquarters, asking for another press conference." Watson stops long enough to take a breath, then he continues, "I want to know the identity of the original leak. I hope it isn't Beck, but I'll see that he loses his job if it is. With Kelly, I spoke to her last night. Supposedly, her intentions were not to cause an uproar with her peers. She was merely showing the work the task force is doing to find this killer."

"Isn't there a back way into police headquarters? We can't use the front entrance." Bob points out.

"Yes, there is. Our ID badges work for the back door too. We've been using it for access to the medical examiner's office, and it's easy in and out." Digger explains.

Watson places a call and speaks to someone on the other end in a not-so-friendly manner with instructions to get rid of the reporters. He doesn't specify how just to make it happen. Watson looks at Bob and says, "we need a press conference today. It will be the same as the other day as I'm not sharing any recent developments. I don't want to share about the halfway house connection yet."

Bob agrees and takes on the responsibility of writing the press release. He says he will have it ready by mid-morning so Watson can set a time to deliver it.

The group slips through the back door with no one noticing. After gathering in the conference room, Larkin expresses his concern about the time spent visiting halfway houses yesterday. He asks for suggestions on alternative ways to handle the visits. All eyes turn downward as the group stares at their phones. No one has a new idea.

"Does anyone have any interesting tales of their visits yesterday?" Larkin asks the group.

Rafter speaks first, "the visits are necessary, but I think we need to visit with each offender. The house managers are not willing or able to divulge sensitive information about their residents. We need to ask every resident the same questions and compile the data. A questionnaire would suffice for this task too. It might be lengthy, but it will be worth it."

Everyone around the table agrees, including Watson. He sits alone in the corner, brooding over the situation with the media. His fingers fly across his phone as he sends a text to someone. He looks up, and all eyes are on him. "I like Rafter's idea. Devise the questionnaire and start making appointments today."

The following two hours were brutal. The group hashes out the questions for the canvass. Some members want other questions added, and others wish to delete some. To satisfy all, the questionnaire is three pages long. A few members rub their necks while others rub their temples because the document is lengthy, but they agree to move forward. They are eager to get started on the meetings.

Just as Digger sat to make calls for their appointments, Larkin got the dreaded call. We wait for his call to finish. "We have another murder. Lancaster Police Department is handling the scene until we arrive. Let's go."

Everyone gathers their things and heads to the vehicles. Larkin leads the convoy. The victim is a Caucasian guy, mid-twenties, and he works as a mechanic. He lived in an apartment two blocks from the mechanic shop where he worked. His co-worker found him when he missed a cookout.

The task force arrives, and they inspect the scene. The apartment complex is older but well maintained, with flowers and shrubbery planted at the entrance and common areas. Parking in the front and rear of the apartments. The complex has a small pool tucked in the corner next to the mailboxes.

Ellie, Digger, and Larkin place booties over their shoes and slap gloves on their hands as they enter the front door. Ellie stops short, and the men bump into her. "Sorry, guys. The smell is powerful. This guy has been dead for a few days."

The men follow her inside and watch as Ellie starts on the left side of the room and then surveys the right side. At every scene, her brain catalogs what her eyes see. She takes no notes during her observation period.

"This is the same killer. He shot the victim point-blank from here." Ellie whispers to Digger and Larkin. "Look at the carving. It is a straight line on the right side of the torso."

Digger stays with Ellie while Larkin inspects the bedroom and bath. "Nothing else of significance in the apartment. It all happened in the kitchen. Once you finish, Ellie, we'll visit with the mechanic shop owner."

We walk the two blocks to the shop. The fresh air feels nice but knowing we added another victim to the growing list, our moods remain solemn. We turn into the shop's parking lot, and it surprises us to see the number of vehicles and motorcycles waiting for service. Ellie glances at the guys, "is this the only mechanic shop in town? It sure is busy."

Larkin and Digger shrug their shoulders, showing their lack of knowledge of the area. Larkin enters the shop first. The trio walks into a small but clean waiting room. An older woman stands behind a counter staring at a computer. "Hi, can I help you, folks?"

Larkin steps in front of the group and produces his badge from his pocket. He explains the reason for their visit. The lady offers, "my husband and I own this place and have for years. Let me get Leon for you." She trots to the outdoor area of the shop without a look back.

The lady enters the waiting area, followed by a guy with a beard and wearing overalls. The man dwarfs the lady, and the group tries not to gawk at his size. "I'm Leon. How can I help you?"

Leon's voice didn't match his size. It shocked the group by how pleasant and mild Leon sounds. Larkin recovers and explains the situation. Leon's eyes teared as he spoke of the victim, Teddy Welsh. Teddy worked at the shop for two years. Leon watched Teddy's life change when he started hanging out with some unfavorable souls. Teddy wouldn't listen to Leon until the cops arrested Teddy for being in a group of guys who stole from the town liquor store. Teddy told Leon he was at the wrong place at the wrong time, and he would stop hanging with those guys. Furthermore, Leon promised Teddy his job would be here after his stint in the halfway house.

Digger stops Leon and inquires, "What is the address of Teddy's halfway house?"

"I'm not sure, but a guy named Chopper runs it."

Chapter 11

Digger nods, and Larkin picks up the questions, "Has Teddy had any new friends stop by the shop recently?"

Leon looks at his wife. "I don't think so," Leon says when his wife exclaims, "Leon, what about the blond-haired boy? You remember with tattoos up and down his arms."

"Oh, I forgot about him. Some guy stopped by the shop several times over the last month. I saw Teddy talking with this guy, standing over at that corner. Afterward, I questioned Teddy, and he said it wasn't anything to worry about."

Leon's wife put her arm around his wide girth and laid her head on his upper arm since her height prevented her from laying it on his shoulder. "I can't believe someone would kill Teddy. He was such a mild-mannered kid. Teddy learned a lot after his arrest, and he said he never wanted to go back inside a jail again."

"Can either of you describe the guy that stopped by the shop?"

While Larkin waited for an answer, Ellie added, "we know he is Caucasian, has blond hair and tattoos. Is there anything special about tattoos?"

The lady shakes her head, but Leon remembers, "one tattoo is colorful, but the other one is a greenish color. I couldn't tell you what the tattoo was because it was all jumbled. The boy wore a cap pulled low almost to his eyebrows, so I couldn't see his eye color. He never spoke to me, hardly looked at me, so I can't comment on an accent either."

Digger compliments the pair in the description. "We appreciate the information you provided. We don't know if this guy had anything to do with Teddy's murder, but we would like to speak with him. Here's my card if he returns."

Larkin passes his card along too. "Thanks for the help. If you remember anything, don't hesitate to call."

The trio leaves the shop and heads back two blocks to the apartment complex. All three survey the surroundings looking for anything to help them. Almost at the lot when Ellie asks, "is there a database of halfway house residents? I'd like to know if this guy ever stayed at a halfway house."

"Good idea, Ellie, but I've never heard of a database like that. It would take too many hours to search each offender's case files. An option is to scan a description to each public defender and see if they recognize anyone like this."

"With our luck, the guy changed his appearance after his halfway house stint," Digger adds with a sad tone. He's frustrated with the lack of movement on the case. Why can't we catch a break?

Larkin plucks his cell phone from his pocket to answer it. The trio stops walking while Larkin speaks with Watson, and they converse for several minutes before the call ends. "Watson's next press conference is at two this afternoon, and he wants us there."

All three leave the apartment complex headed for police headquarters and the subsequent press conference. TV cameras and people crowd the steps. Ellie slips in the back door of headquarters to drop off notebooks and such. When she exits, she spots Beck leaning against a light pole on the other side of the street. She tries to locate Digger or Larkin, but she can't find them in the crowd, and Watson prepares for his speech. Ellie can't believe the number of people that have shown up to witness this conference.

Watson dresses the part as Bob checks on the microphones and straightens the podium. As he looks over the crowd, he locks eyes with Kelly Knight. She gives him a slight nod of the head. He returns the nod. Watson looks around for his team and finds Digger standing with Larkin to his left. Watson grows concerned as he doesn't see Ellie. A wave of his hand brings Digger to his side. "Find Ellie. We spotted Beck across the street."

Digger trots back to his spot next to Larkin. "Beck is in the area, and we need to find Ellie."

The duo splits, and each takes a side of the stage area. Almost to the end, Ellie stands to survey the pile of people. "There you are, Digger. I have looked everywhere for you."

With a sigh of relief, Digger grabs her hand, "Beck is in the area, and I had bad thoughts running through my mind."

"I saw him leaning against the light pole across the street. That's when I jumped in the crowd of people."

"Good thinking. Let's go. Watson waits for us." The two strode off hand in hand while Digger sends Larkin a text confirming Ellie is safe.

The press release was nothing but brilliant. Bob is a word genius. He says things without entirely saying anything. After the conference is over, the reporters seem satisfied. Kelly was privy to this morning's murder information as Bob handed her a question to ask about the murder. It went off without a hitch. The media were pleasant today, which was odd.

Just as the conference ends, a loud noise sounds from the street. All heads turn and watch as a TV van explodes. People scream as they run from the area. The group heads to the truck. Injured people litter the sidewalk. Some with lacerations and shrapnel wounds, one with a broken arm, and others with bruises. The TV van was from a station in Philadelphia. No one was in the van, but the debris field was vast.

Emergency vehicles arrive on the scene within minutes. The group sets up a staging and triage area in a shaded area next to the police headquarters. Police investigators converge on the wounded, and they ask questions of those able to answer. Sirens blare as ambulances pull up in a line and park at the steps. One after the other, they pull away with another patient, heading to the local hospital.

Officer Rafter was on the scene when the explosion rocked the conference. Luckily, he had just passed the area. He suffered a fall from the blast but nothing more than a bruised elbow. He works to help others when Digger walks over to him and asks him about the explosion. Officer Rafter also admits to seeing Beck across the street, but he can't put Beck beside the truck. Rafter was too busy with crowd control. No one expected the crowd to be this large.

Digger walks halfway up the steps and surveys the area. There are dozens of emergency vehicles lining the roadway and people milling about. He doesn't see Beck anywhere. Digger watches as the bomb squad pulls in behind the smoldering TV van.

The task force leaves the area and heads upstairs to discuss the situation. After roll call, Watson begins the meeting. "Thank goodness we're safe, except for Rafter's elbow. It could have been devastating. I think we all know they spotted Beck in the area before the press conference. I notified the bomb squad of his situation, and they will take over the investigation from here. They might call on us for extra information."

Larkin stands and addresses the group about this morning's murder. He shares the information they received from Leon and his wife. The murder scene matches the others. Larkin describes Teddy's visitor, and he explains his intentions of emailing the description to the public defender's office on the off chance they recognize it. They hope the tattoos help with recognition.

Some task force members have upcoming appointments with the halfway house residents, so they skipped out on the rest of the meeting. Ellie takes the latest carving and draws the picture on a notecard. She is determined to figure out what the killer is drawing. Why one carving at a time? With Teddy's visitor, she assumes it somehow involved him. Whether he pulled the trigger or lured the guy to his death, he is involved. Why else would he show up at the shop without a vehicle?

Ellie leans over to Digger, "how did Teddy's visitor get to the shop? Leon didn't mention a vehicle or motorcycle."

Larkin hears the question, "Um. I would like to know that myself. How about I call Leon? If the visitor walked to the shop, he would have to live around there, right?"

"Not exactly. He could have driven and parked it down the street and walked into the shop. Especially if he was hiding the vehicle." Digger points out.

"Thanks for killing my idea, Digger. Does it matter if we know how he arrived at the shop?" Larkin asks with his eyebrows bunched.

Ellie glances at Digger, "if you state it like that, it doesn't matter."

Everyone sits back in their chairs. Ellie leans her head back while Digger plays with the note cards. He shuffles them a time or two like a deck of cards. Spreads them out on the table, stares at the cards, picks them up and does it all over again. After several minutes, he holds the stack in one hand and flips the cards like a book. He studies the pictures as the cards flip. Digger jumps up, "I know what the picture is. Watch this." He strolls to the whiteboard.

With a blue marker, Digger follows the pictures in order of the murders. An image comes to fruition. The killer is drawing the Scales of Justice. Digger and his discovery amazed everyone. He admits it was pure luck and the old-fashioned flip book. The group asks to see how Digger did it. Digger gives the group a lesson on flip books. "I made flip books as a kid, and I should have thought of it earlier."

Ellie studies the picture, "how many pieces are missing from our picture?"

Digger looks at Ellie and understands the question after a mental pause. "It looks like there might be a vertical straight line here and, of course, the other side of the scale."

Watson beats Larkin by saying, "how many more murders are we looking at? I don't want to draw the complete picture, guys. We need to get this guy."

"It's several, Watson. But we'll catch him before he finishes. We have a vague description of a guy that visited Teddy, this morning's victim. We'll email the description to our three public defenders and see if they recognize the guy." Larkin explains as he powers up his laptop. Watson watches as Larkin completes the task. Now, the wait is on. The group is aware the visitor might have been just a visitor, but, strangely, the guy didn't have a vehicle, or he hid it.

Bob and Rafter study a laptop and whisper amongst themselves. Ellie nods toward the two, hoping Digger will acknowledge them, but Watson is curious too, and he asks instead. "What are two looking at so intently?"

With his laptop in hand, Rafter faces it toward the group. "Bob had the brilliant idea to check camera footage around headquarters hoping to spot the culprit behind the bombing. This is the first camera angle. Nothing so far, but we have nine cameras to check. Does anyone feel like watching a few videos?"

Everyone agrees to watch camera footage of the area, hoping to gain on the perpetrator. Digger's camera points to the side of headquarters, where they staged a triage spot. Before the conference, he watches as people walk back and forth across the lawn. TV personnel set up and tested their cameras and microphones. Nothing appears out of the ordinary until the van explodes. Digger gets an up-close, view of the carnage. Most of the truck is out of sight at this angle.

"Who has the camera next to the one I'm watching? If I had a little more visual of the van, I might have something. This video shows the destruction. If you have a queasy stomach, I suggest skipping this one." Digger comments.

Bob and Rafter check the list, "I have it, and it's running. Come on over and join me." Bob suggests.

The video is close to the end, "Have you seen the van yet, Bob? It should have been in the previous video."

"No, it hasn't shown yet. I can see part of the lawn so far."

Digger leans back and studies the video. The van is missing, and it makes little sense. Digger restarts his video and plays it until the front of the van is in view. Then he looks at Bob's video and compares the two. A portion of the road is missing. It's a blank space.

Bob's video ends, and he stares at Digger with a blank look. "Why wasn't the van in this video? This one follows yours."

Digger explains the blank spot in the video. He cued his video at the precise moment the blast occurred, and he pointed out the truck. Then he does the same with Bob's. When the time stamp matches, the angles don't. "My question is, does Beck know about this blank space? It would be a perfect cover."

Watson shakes his head, not knowing how to answer. He stands and paces the room while glancing out the window. The bomber didn't know the press conference would be today, let alone the time. It was an impromptu blast which means the blasting device was something you can get at a hardware store. He plucks his phone from his pocket and dials the bomb squad captain.

The captain describes what Watson feared. The bomb-making ingredients were homemade. There is no way to trace where the bomber purchased the components, but he suggested checking the local stores. The time between the press conference announcement and the actual conference wasn't long, so the bomber had to move quickly to carry it out today.

After Watson shares the captain's ideas with the group, they put a plan together. Since some of their people were meeting with offenders, Larkin suggests using a few patrol officers. They can make stops and ask the clerks if they remember someone purchasing these listed items.

The reconstructionist calls Digger to advise she received the skulls, and they are intact. She will begin first thing in the morning, and results will be within forty-eight hours. Digger reminds her to make the reconstructions older, around sixty-five or seventy. He can't explain the reason behind the age but suspects it relates to the original set of skeletons.

Back to the bombing, the group agrees to hold off on visiting offenders for the day. The explosion rattled them, and Rafter stopped by the hospital for an x-ray. His elbow has doubled in size since we began watching the videos.

Bob announces he's driving Rafter to the hospital. Larkin will see the rest of the group get a lift to the hotel. The group will reconvene in the morning and work on the offender's list and any replies to Larkin's email about Teddy's visitor.

As Ellie prepares for bed, her cell phone rings. Without a thought, she answers it. Her heart drops to her stomach. "Why are you calling me? You know I have nothing to say. Detective Beck, we are over. You must understand and move forward with your life."

Beck replies with garbled words as if he is drunk. He admits to loving Ellie and refuses to go on living without her. Beck didn't know how much she meant to him until he saw her again. Beck ends the call by telling Ellie he will see her tomorrow.

Startled by the call, Ellie taps on Digger's door. He opens it, and Ellie's expression gives away her uneasiness. She walks in and shares the phone call with Digger. "What did he mean when he said he would see me tomorrow, Digger? Is he following us? This guy is scaring me."

"I can't answer for Detective Beck and his meanings for a statement, but I can promise you will not be alone tomorrow for a minute. It's late. Stay here with me, and we'll discuss with Watson and Larkin in the morning."

"Didn't Watson say they suspended Beck from the force until IA conducted their investigation? If that's so, he shouldn't be at police headquarters anyway, right?"

Digger pauses, then answer, "I heard he is off duty pending the outcome of the investigation."

"I'll be okay in my room, but can we leave the connecting door ajar?" Ellie sheepishly asks.

Digger chuckles and waits until Ellie is in bed, then he turns and leaves the door open as he walks to his bed. He lays in bed, wondering why Beck has his sights set on Ellie after all these years. Is Ellie the reason he flipped out? Other people said Beck acted strangely before Ellie arrived on the scene, but he sounds worse off now.

Chapter 12

Overnight the weather turns violent with lightning, thunder, and howling winds. Ellie couldn't sleep if she wanted to with the outside racket. Propped up in bed, she studies the murder files. She reviews her notes from each scene. Teddy's visitor would play right into the killer's hand since he gains entry to the victim's home before shooting them. Also, the blood evidence proves the killer is left-handed. The group has yet to search for a left-handed offender.

With a blank piece of paper, Ellie jots notes of new ideas and directions for the investigation. Now they know the picture, that part of the investigation is over, and all concentration centers on finding the killer.

The killer is left-handed, and friends or acquaintances of the victims. They met in a halfway house or jail and befriended them. That is how the killer gains access to the residences. Without knowing the killer's age, checking arrest records for Pittsburgh will be impossible, and the records don't include hand preference.

Ellie throws her head back in disgust, knowing this killer is cold and calculating. The worst of the bunch and the hardest to find. She knows they'll catch him. They always do, but how many more bodies must pile up before it happens?

The morning is gray and cloudy with drops of rain. No one has much to say on the drive to police headquarters. The group is tired of the daily rides and the conference room. When they enter, Kelly

Knight waves them a good morning. Watson walks up to her, "what are you doing here, and how did you get permission to be in the conference room alone?"

Kelly smiles a seductive smile toward Watson, "Oh, I'm not alone. Office Rafter is fetching coffee."

"Fetching, Kelly. Really? Isn't fetching a little demeaning?" Watson asks with a smirk on his face.

"I guess it is a little. I should have used a different word. My apologies. Can we start this conversation over? My intentions were not to disturb you today. I'm here to offer my services."

With her comment, every eyebrow in the room lifts. "What do you mean, Kelly?"

"My TV cameraman has video footage of the blast. I think you want to sit for this. Can you stop to see it now? We need to get to the station."

Watson glances around the room. "Sure, we can. Everyone grab a seat."

The cameraman hooks up a laptop so he can show the video of the blast. The group waits as the guys search for the correct time. They notice the cameraman has an awful habit of clicking his tongue when he finds something. After three tongue clicks, he swivels around in his chair, and the video begins.

Digger scans the group to make sure all eyes are on the video. Kelly makes eye contact, and she winks at him. He doesn't know how to take the flirting, so he turns his attention back to the show. The camera pans about the area several times when a younger guy in a dark jacket walks up beside the TV van. He vanishes for a moment then pops back up into the video. The guy is faceless. We only see his back and the back of his head. He has longer sandy-blond hair. That's our only description.

"It's not much, but it's more than what we had. It doesn't appear Beck had anything to do with the blast, and that is an excellent thing." Watson continues, "Kelly. Come on. I'll walk you out."

As Watson and Kelly leave, the group keeps their eyes on him. He places his hand in the small of Kelly's back. Rafter whistles low and faces Bob. "Is there anything we need to know about those two?"

Bob shakes his head. "I am pleading the fifth." He walks out of the conference room toward the break room.

Later in the day, the other group members arrive with their questionnaires in hand. Two members have missing offenders, and the halfway houses don't have an address on two guys. So we turned those into the detective unit, hoping they could find the missing guys. One halfway house manager out in the suburbs told us Chopper's house is the oldest in town. Most severe offenders, not necessarily in crime but personalities, start at his home. He is strict. After his house, the next in line is Terry Wilson's.

"Terry Wilson. Isn't he the guy that wasn't at the house when we stopped by?" Digger asks as he faces Ellie and Larkin.

Larkin pulls his notes and looks up, "you're correct, Digger. We spoke with a young kid who is Terry's gatekeeper. It sounds like we need to take another crack at this Terry Wilson guy. We'll stop by his halfway house in the morning, then come here for a briefing. Watson let me know the brass is getting nervous with the number of killings. They're looking for results."

Another day ends with nothing to show for it. This case agitates Ellie. She doesn't feel she can contribute any more than she has already. What can she do? She gets up from her chair and pulls the files from her bag. She lays them out on the bed with a photo of the Scales of Justice. Why would someone carve bits and pieces of this picture into another person?

Ellie takes a pad of paper and begins profiling the killer. The first item on her list is his hand preference. He is left-handed. It helps the coroner also confirmed a left-handed person did the carvings. Odds are the killer, and the carver is the same person. The killer would be in his mid-twenties, unmarried, rambler. He also spent time in prison or jail. With the use of the carvings, he's not happy with the justice system. For whatever reason, he feels they slighted him either in sentence or place of incarceration, and his killings are revenge.

Digger's cell phone lights up with a call. He answers and listens to Ellie explain her profile. "Can I walk fifteen steps and see you? It would be more pleasant than a phone call."

A chuckle escapes Ellie's throat. "Come on over."

Two seconds later, Digger walks into her room and sits in a chair at her bedside. "Show me what you have. I have bones spread out on my bed, and you have blood spatter. It doesn't say much for us, does it?"

"I didn't mean to take you away from your bones, Digger. A thought came to mind, and I want to share it."

"Go ahead. Let's hear it." Digger waves his hand as he gives her the floor.

Ellie shares her profile of the killer right down to the revenge aspect. Lines crease Digger's forehead as he studies her profile. "Also, Digger, Leon's description of Teddy's visitor favors our alleged bomber."

"What? No one caught that this afternoon. Where would we be without you? You always remember the nitty-gritty things. Your profile is spot on. Now, to find this guy. One question is, does the killer work alone?"

"Yes. There is only one spot in the blood pattern that could perpetuate space for the shooter. If someone else were there, they would have to be outside the door or maybe a driver. There is no way two people were in the kill zone. The killer also polices his brass. We have yet to find a spent cartridge at the scene."

"Wait until Larkin hears this! No one has mentioned the cartridge, either. Since I can't compete with your brain tonight, I'm going to bed. Sleep tight. See you in the morning." Digger walks by and kisses Ellie.

Smiling, Ellie lays down to sleep. Her mind is empty after her brainstorming session. Just as she is dozing, her phone rings. She assumes it is Digger, but she guesses wrong. "Marshall, I asked you not to call me anymore. Please know I have nothing to say. Take it up with Watson. He decides on the lead detectives for his case. Good night, Beck."

Ellie places her phone face first so the screen will not light the room. Why does he keep calling me? He said I was to see him today, but it didn't happen either. Ellie stews over Beck and what could cause him to act in this manner. She wonders if he is married and if the pair are having issues at home. Whatever it is, Ellie is at peace with her decision to stay with Digger. She turns over and drifts into a restful sleep.

The threesome dropped in early at the halfway house looking for Terry Wilson. The same younger guy greets them like last time. "Terry is out this morning. I'll let him know you stopped in again."

Larkin shakes his head from side to side and says, "that will not work this time. We'll wait until Terry returns, or I can have code enforcement stop by and see how things are going here."

"I'll give Terry a call and make sure he is on his way back from the grocery store." Larkin stands next to the guy while he calls so he can watch him dial the number. He heard Terry answer. "Terry is checking out now. He said to give him ten minutes. I'll show you around while we wait."

The guy waves his hand, and all three stand, then following in a single file. Terry's house is smaller than Chopper's, but it's neater. There's not a speck of dust anywhere. While the guy walks us around, he tells us Terry is older and spent one year in prison. Five years after they released him, he opened this halfway house. He has been clean and sober for fifty years.

Terry's gatekeeper continues by telling us Terry does nothing else but this. He has five guys help at the house, and the state allows him to pick his tenants. His tenants are less lethal, meaning they want another chance in life.

Ellie whispers to Digger, "this might not be the place for our killer if this guy is telling the truth."

"We'll know soon enough. I would bet Terry is entering the kitchen door." Digger nods his head toward the door.

After a man places full grocery bags on the counter, he strolls into the room and introduces himself as Terry Wilson. "What can I do for you?"

Larkin steps up, shows his badge, and explains the reason for our visits. Terry admitted to hearing about the murders but didn't realize a halfway house connected them.

"We're suspecting the killer didn't like their sentence handed down by a judge or maybe the prison or jail. Since all victims were from halfway houses in town, we surmise our killer stayed at one as well."

Terry's eyebrows grew together, "A killer in a halfway house is unimaginable. My tenants are learning to re-enter society. A few have counselors for alcohol or drug rehab, but I handpicked those guys. If the killer had a propensity to violence in prison, I don't see how a judge placed him in a center. Offenders placed in a halfway house are those that have committed victimless crimes. I can't imagine it involving one of my guys."

"If not one of yours, where would you send us next?"

"Chopper's house. Have you been there yet? We consider his boys the roughest. Chopper and his mentors are strict in managing his guys, but you never know if one slips the cracks."

"Thanks, Terry, for your time. You've been a substantial help. Have a wonderful day." Larkin states and Ellie and Digger acknowledge the same.

"Back to Chopper's we go, guys," Larkin says as the group climbs in the vehicle.

As Larkin pulls to Chopper's curb, Digger's phone rings. His heartbeat speeds up when he recognizes the number. He answers and listens as the caller describes the reconstructions. As the call ends, Digger tells Ellie and Larkin the skull reconstructions are back. He opens his email and glances at the pictures. Digger is so proud to know Ruby Holbrook. Ruby and Digger met years ago at a conference as Ruby was starting her new career. Ruby is detailed and always listens to Digger's idea of the skull.

"Look at these pictures. These are phenomenal. Now, we figure out who they are. What do you think, Larkin?" Digger's excitement is contagious.

"The skulls look like actual persons, Digger. How did she know to age them?" Larkin inquires.

"I suggested the older age based on the age of the original skeletons. These two might be local as well, and they might be a relation to our killer. I've searched every database I know for a young person with the surname Teeter, and nothing shows. So, I am at a standstill with identification."

Larkin stares at the pictures of the skulls. "What are the odds Watson will let us use Kelly Knight? She can report on the bones and show the skulls on TV for us."

Ellie clears her throat. "Watson didn't seem happy to see Kelly last time. You can ask him but prepare yourself for a tongue lashing if he doesn't like the idea."

As Larkin hands Digger's phone back to him, Larkin plucks his phone from his pants pocket. "I say we go back to the office and visit with Watson. I'll call him and make sure he is there."

Larkin dials Watson, and he answers on the first ring. They speak for thirty seconds. With a titled head and creased brows, Larkin turns to face the duo. "Watson is meeting Kelly for brunch. He asks us to meet him at the office. Kelly requested this meeting with Watson, so he is skeptical if she will help."

"Interesting development. I bet Bob knows what's going on with Watson. Let's go back to the office and prepare for Watson. We need several glossy prints of the skulls to distribute amongst the state."

Larkin pulls away from the curb and drives to the office. Headquarters is quiet as they enter from the back of the building. Bob works alone in the conference room when the trio comes. "Hey, guys, any recent information on the murders?"

"Depends on which murders you are referring to, Bob. I have photos of the skull reconstructions." Digger shares.

"Can I see them? Being a reconstructionist is fascinating to me."

Digger hands his phone to Bob with the email open. Bob studies the pictures and says, "This is simply amazing. The detail is uncanny. How did the reconstructionist know to age the skulls?"

"I've answered the same question more than once today. I suggested the age. These two skulls were older than the original skulls when compared. They were all killed in the same manner. I think these skulls might be a relation to the Teeter's, but I have no way of knowing for sure."

Bob hands Digger's phone back as Watson enters the room. His face is a myriad of expressions. "What's up, Watson? Are you okay?" Bob asks.

"Well, where do I start? Kelly invited me to brunch, and why I thought we were because becoming friends is beyond me. We have enjoyed cordial phone calls over the past few days, not that any of you need to know. As soon as I sit at the table, she prods me about the connections to the halfway houses. Of course, I try to change the subject, but with Kelly, that's impossible. I finally gave up and told her I had a meeting, and I would call later." Watson sinks into a chair and sighs.

Ellie can tell it bothers Watson. "I know she flusters you, but what if we could use her services? We might satisfy her for a little while." Ellie offers.

Watson turns at looks at Ellie, then makes eye contact with Bob, Digger, and Larkin. Digger takes the floor, "I've received the skulls from the reconstructionist. They are remarkable. Here are the photos." Digger hands over the recently printed glossy prints of the two skulls. "Before you ask, I suggested the age for the reconstructionist based on the age of the other two skulls," Digger explains as the rest of the group chuckles.

"Why is everyone laughing?"

"Because each of them asked me the same question today at different times. So, I answered your question without you having to ask it." Digger grins.

"Let me get this straight. You want me to ask Kelly if she wants a lead story on the skulls? Are you all sure you want her involved? She is related to a piranha. Once she gets her teeth into something, she doesn't let go." Watson states.

"We need to showcase the skulls and see if someone recognizes them. The police department will handle the calls, and they can farm the most important to me." Digger adds.

"Okay. I'll call her." Watson agrees as he lowers his chin to his chest. He feels defeated. He thought Kelly might be an excellent catch for him, but she uses him for information.

Ellie brings everyone's attention to her. "I have a new profile of our killer I'd like to share if now is an agreeable time."

All heads nod, so she begins. She repeats her conversation with Digger to the group. Larkin is in awe at Ellie's aptitude for profiling. Watson sends compliments her way as well.

Bob jots notes from the profile in his book. He circles a few of them. "How should we handle this information? Do we have a list of the mentors or workers from the halfway houses in town? If you are positive, this is a revenge-killing spree, then the killer is staying at a halfway house, has stayed at one, or works at one now."

"I agree with Bob," Larkin states. "Does the state have a list of who works at these facilities, or is it something the house managers handle on their own? Does anyone know?"

Heads shake around the room, and Digger raises his hand, "Terry Wilson will help us on this one. I'll call him." Digger dug out his phone number and dialed.

Terry answers on the second ring. Digger questions Terry about the mentors or workers for the halfway houses, and he asks if the houses operate in the same manner as workers?

The government backs the halfway houses as long as they follow protocols set forth by the state. Terry hires and fires his staff. They must go through a background check that includes criminal and meet specific criteria to become a worker. Terry confirms there is no database for halfway house workers. Each house handles its own.

Chapter 13

The group determines the only way get a list of workers is to call each halfway house in the city and request it from the managers or owners. Larkin assigns this duty to several patrol officers on the task force.

Watson advises Kelly will stop by this afternoon to discuss the skulls. She also wants information on the halfway house connection. I've complained about sharing anything until we get more information. "Digger, can you placate Kelly with an interview on bone recovery and how you work with a reconstructionist?"

As he stammers, Digger says, "I suppose so. Although I don't want my photo on TV, I'll be happy to add to her story, but I want the skulls identified."

"I know the end game, but this lady is relentless. She doesn't stop. You have the perfect story to hold her interest for a day or two. We need more information from the halfway houses, and I don't want to jeopardize our working relationship with Chopper or Terry."

Bob speaks up, "I'll help Digger with Kelly. We can spin the words to say whatever we need." This satisfies Watson and Digger. Although Digger's mind runs at 100 MPH as he worries about his conversation with Kelly.

After lunch, the group works on updating the murder book. When Kelly appears at the doorway, everyone turns toward her when she clears her throat. "You sure are busy this afternoon. May I enter?" Kelly asks.

Watson jumps up and greets Kelly and then ushers her inside to a seat next to Digger. Digger raises his eyebrows as he turns to face Kelly. She starts, "I hear you need help to identify someone. I'm here to help."

Digger looks at Bob and back at Kelly. Bob stands and introduces himself to Kelly. Then, he suggests the three of them go next door to a private room where they can talk uninterrupted.

Digger follows the trail to a small office next door to the conference room with photos in hand. "Kelly, please sit behind the desk. It might help if you intend to take notes and such." Bob suggests.

Kelly sits with her back to the window, so she can face the men. "Let's start from the beginning. Watson said you have a story to tell." With her pad and pen on the table, she turns her attention to Digger.

Bob and Digger cringe but continue, "We need these reconstructed skulls identified." Digger places them on the desk, then leans back. This lady makes him antsy.

Kelly picks up the photos and studies them. "May I keep these? I can return them after the story airs."

"Sure." Digger looks at Bob for assurance. Once Bob nods, Digger begins the story of how he became involved with this set of unidentified skeletons. Kelly asks pointed questions about tools for this type of work, length of time to recover bones, transportation of bones, and reconstructionist and their duties. While Kelly jots notes, she writes the story in her head.

"This is fascinating, Digger. May I quote you in the story?"

"My name is Chet Collins if you must quote me. I'd prefer no photos of me, just the skulls. My goal is to get these people identified and properly buried. The police department set up a tip line if your viewers recognize this couple. Here is the number." Digger passes a note to Kelly with the number written on it.

"Believe me. You'll have callers. They may not know the identity, but you'll have callers." Kelly adds with a chuckle as she accepts the phone number from Digger. Kelly looks up at Digger and asks, "Tell me how the skulls relate to the carving murders."

His wide eyes give Kelly what she wants. She shocks Bob and Digger. "You know these skulls are related, don't you?" Kelly prods.

"No, actually, I don't know. It's a coincidence they found the skulls at the same time this killer is loose, but I'm not big on coincidences." Digger hopes to leave the explanation at that.

"What are the names of the original skeletons you found at the same discovery site?" Kelly still picks for information.

Bob provides the names of the original skeletons from his notes. He explains there are no photos since we confirmed identification through other means.

Kelly again, "through other means, Bob. What does that mean?"

The explanation continues as Digger and Bob explain the house and Digger's idea the skeletons were the deceased owners of the house.

Now, Kelly's face shows signs of shock. Her eyes are wide with her hand on her mouth, "Digger, how did you determine the owners of the house were buried in their own crawl space?"

Bob laughs as Digger answers the question for the fourth time today. Digger sits there and wonders why no one else can figure that out. In his brain, it is perfectly logical.

Kelly asks for a few minutes to compile her notes. She doesn't want to leave anything on the table. After a break, Kelly is excited to say the story will make the six o'clock news. She'll report it herself. She stands and shakes hands with Digger and Bob and waves her hand over her head as the guys watch her sashay out the door.

"That is one hour of my life I'll never get back. I hope it was worth it." Digger stands and stretches and walks to the break room for coffee.

"Kelly is something else," Bob speaks more to himself than anyone else, but Digger heard every word.

Bob pours cream into his coffee without ever looking at the cup, "Uh, Bob. Are you having coffee with your cream?"

His head swivels on his neck, "What, Digger? I missed what you said."

"I know you did, Bob. Your mind is on Kelly Knight. You can watch her on the news tonight and stare at her while she gives her report." Digger says and laughs on his way to the conference room.

The team members wait with anticipation to hear the result of Kelly's meeting. Digger walks in, still laughing at Bob. "What is so funny, Digger? Please tell me everything went okay with Kelly?"

"It went fine. I'll let Bob explain my laughter. It was at his expense."

Officer Rafter stands at the table when Bob enters. "So, Bob. Why did Digger come back laughing? He told us you would explain it."

All eyes are on Bob as his face turns red. "It was nothing. Digger caught me at a weak moment."

Watson looked away then up at Bob, "Ah, the Kelly syndrome. Well, Bob, this is the first time I've seen you react to a lady like this. It's nice to know I'm not alone." The group breaks out in laughter.

Ellie suggests an early dinner so they can watch the newscast. She hopes the news report provides leads to identify the skulls. Digger is obsessed with identifying every recovered skull. To date, he has no unidentified skulls. In his profession, that is an accomplishment.

The group opts for a sports bar down the block from police headquarters. They enjoy a walk to the bar since the weather is beautiful. Larkin steps to the hostess and explains their predicament about needing a TV. The hostess sits the team in the back with a TV, and Larkin controls the sound.

At six sharp, the TV shows Kelly Knight in a bright royal blue blouse and hot pink lipstick. Bob and Watson take a breath. Kelly is nothing but masterful in her delivery of the skulls. The story details are brief, and the outline is superb. Once Kelly concludes her report, she flashes the tip line phone number and repeats it twice.

Digger raises his eyebrows at Kelly's professionalism. "I didn't know she would spin the story together like that. I expect plenty of calls just because she read the number."

Watson spoke next, "We're not doing anything with the tip line tonight. If we receive a call that warrants a closer look, we'll get the list tomorrow. Tonight, you rest and be ready to work tomorrow. Also, has anyone noticed we haven't had a murder in a while? I'm not sure what to make of this killer's timetable."

"The murder has probably already occurred. We just haven't received word yet. If he's true to his pattern, the victim has been off work for a few days, so no one has discovered the body. Give it time, Watson. The killer isn't finished yet. He still has a few more carvings before he completes his picture.

Everyone shakes their head over Ellie's statement. They want to capture this guy before he completes the picture. There aren't many more victims to go before the killer finishes with the image, and Kelly isn't privy to the information. She has the capability of butchering the police and the FBI over these murders. The group agrees to keep Kelly at arm's length to control the information she reveals.

"If we identify these skulls, what about asking Kelly to showcase the description of Teddy's visitor? We can say he is a person of interest instead of using the word suspect." Ellie proposes. "Also, I checked with the lab, and the DNA from the blood is from the victim. No other DNA was found at any scene. The lab has a smeared fingerprint, but they need a print to compare it too."

Watson contemplates his reply. "I agree on letting Kelly showcase the description, but I would like to give the skulls a three-day chance at this before we let Kelly hit the airwaves again. On the DNA, no surprise there. The killer knows how to protect himself from DNA matches. I saw the fingerprint in the lab. It's a positive smear. I'm not sure if we can match it. There are only a few points from the print."

With the day starting at eight, the group splits for the night. Digger and Ellie walk hand in hand to the headquarters parking lot. They ride to the hotel with Bob and Watson in silence. Everyone dreams of going home and getting their life back. Serial killers take so much time from those who track them. They sleep when they have downtime.

The evening was pleasant, but Digger has trouble paying attention to those around him. His mind on the tip line and what it might offer. He lays in bed with thoughts swirling in his mind, but Digger wakes to a new morning, eager to hear of the calls from the tip line. He walks into the elevator with a grin on his face. "Good morning, folks," Digger says to the group. All acknowledge him with a grunt. "Is everyone still sleepy?" Digger prods.

"Coffee. Just need coffee." Bob retorts.

After breakfast, Bod drives the group to headquarters. Digger and Watson head for the office, operating the tip line. With wide eyes and lifted brows, the men flip through stacks of messages. Some are bogus, just by the caller's name, but a few seem legit. Overnight officers visited two callers and took their statements.

Larkin walks up behind the duo and asks about the statements. The patrol officer hands the reports to Larkin for review. "Guys, follow me. We might have something."

The trio enters the conference room with Rafter and Ellie already seated. Larkin peruses the reports and says, "two reports from two different callers are

159

similar. They are almost certain they recognize these skulls. One caller owns a grocery store east of the city, and the other is a restaurant owner in the same area. We'll visit each person today as the callers didn't give us a name for our skulls. Just the notion they had seen them years ago in the area."

"Amazing. Someone recognizes them at this age. Although the facial structure is still intact, we added lines and gray hair for the age they would be now. I still believe the skulls belong to someone in the Teeter family. This confirms it. If the people visited the same area, they were here to see the Teeter's."

Ellie looks at Digger and offers, "If you feel that, let me check my genealogy database. I can try to find the Teeter's parents. I'll work your angle while you check up on the callers."

Watson nods in agreement as he explains the morning work schedule. "Ellie, you are on the Teeter's genealogy while Digger and Larkin can follow up on the callers. As a reminder, we have another press conference at two this afternoon. Let's meet around one to get updates from everyone."

With her laptop in hand, Ellie finds a quiet corner of the conference room and begins the tedious searches in the Teeter's lineage. These searches are time consuming, but they sometimes work.

Larkin and Digger make appointments to meet with both callers this morning. They grab their gear and trot to the elevator. The first appointment is in fifteen minutes, and the drive is twenty. Since Larkin is a local, his street knowledge is priceless.

He maneuvers the vehicle along the side streets, across major roads into the area in sixteen minutes.

"I'm impressed, Larkin. You accomplished it without a scratch." Digger says as he tries to get his legs back under him. "You know how to handle a vehicle." Digger shakes off the adrenaline rush on his way to the door.

"Thanks, Digger. Nothing out of the ordinary for me." Larkin shows the way to the restaurant. The owner requested the duo show before the lunch crowd. As they enter, the smell of oregano, basil, parsley, and pasta envelopes them. Both men's stomach growls as they enjoy the aroma.

The owner approaches them from the kitchen. "Welcome. Let's sit here out of earshot of my kitchen staff. Would you care for something to drink?"

Both men decline the offer, and Larkin is the first to pull his notebook out of his bag. He also lays the caller's report on the table. "We have a few follow-up questions about your report regarding the skulls. First, how long has it been since you have seen these people you recognize?"

"Oh my. That's hard to say. I've owned this restaurant for forty years this month. If I must guess, I'd say ten to fifteen years. Those people would always come in with another couple. I'm an excellent judge of families, and I always assumed they were family. The ladies constantly chatted while the men drank beer. Then one day, I realized I hadn't seen either couple, then I stopped looking for them."

"Did you ever get their names?" Digger prods.

"No, not directly. I might have had their names on a credit card slip, but those are long gone. Their favorite server passed last year from cancer. She might have known their names. The younger couple used to eat here once a week."

"So, the older couple might not be from around here, right? They were visiting from out of town." Larkin inquires.

The restaurant owner nods in affirmative. "I wish I could be more help, gentlemen."

Larkin and Digger stand and shake hands with the owner and leave for the next appointment. They have plenty of time to make this trip, so they stop at the Teeter's house. Digger exits the vehicle and leans against it as he stares at the house. No one has demolished it yet because of the bones. Yellow crime scene tape covers the doors of the home. It doesn't appear anyone has been inside since they discovered the bones.

After a few minutes of solitude, the duo heads to the grocery store for their second meeting. The grocery store owner waited as they walked in the door. After introductions, she led them to a small office in the back of the store. The owner confirms the couple would frequent the store with a younger couple. While the men bought beer, the ladies would purchase other things. The two couples shopped in the store two times a month or more, depending on the season. They didn't share names, and she agreed with the timetable from the restaurant owner. She also mentions the older couple seemed to be from out of town. They always rode with the younger ones.

Digger slides into the passenger seat and says, "our skulls are from out of town. Does Kelly have access to a national station that would share the skulls?" He glances at Larkin, waiting for an answer.

"She might. We can speak to her this afternoon. Watson is showing the skull photos today at the conference too. They are waiting on us for lunch. Watson catered sandwiches for the team." The drive back to the office was slower than the first trip. For that, Digger was grateful.

Larkin updated the team during a working lunch because they needed time to share before the conference, so Bob had ample time to write the press release. Things fall into place for Bob, and he constructs another brilliant release.

Watson walks to the podium with the photos in hand. He slides them under his notes. The skulls will be the last topic. He begins with an update on the investigation, and he acknowledges a person of interest. He floats a brief description of the guy and moves on. Just as he is about to change the topic, a reporter yells out a question about halfway houses.

In mid-sentence, Watson changes tactics. He dives into the information relating to the halfway houses. Bob crafted a fabulous comeback on the halfway house connection. It said there is a possibility of a relationship but no guarantees. The task force is investigating all options.

The skull photos flap in the breeze as Watson holds them above his head. Everyone's attention is on Watson as he offers something new. He gave Kelly Knight credit for her news report last night, but he wants to share it with the rest of the media since the couple is out of town. Bob stands next to Watson and holds the photos of the skulls while the press asks questions and takes pictures for their news report. Watson smiles.

At the end of the conference, Detective Beck yells from the back of the group. "The FBI is no good at solving murders. They should have left the investigation to the local police." Beck continues his tirade by blaming the lack of leadership on FBI Special Agent Watson. He emphasized the special agent part of Watson's title.

Beck makes eye contact with Ellie as Ellie shakes her head in disbelief. He walks to Ellie's side as she tries to back away from him. He grabs her wrist and tells her in front of the crowd they should have made it work.

Officer Rafter, Larkin, and Digger cut through the crowd to reach Ellie. They try to talk him down by releasing Ellie. Beck waves his police-issued weapon in the air, yelling for everyone to back away. As Beck stares into Ellie's eyes, he places the gun to his chin.

Chapter 14

Ellie's eyes dart from Beck to Digger and back again. She struggles with Beck's strength on her wrist. "Let me go, Marshall," Ellie says in a soft voice. She uses her free hand to try to release Beck's fingers from her wrist. "Come on. We can step away from the crowd and talk things through. Please, Marshall." She tugs her arm, hoping he releases her, but his grip becomes firmer, and he draws her closer.

Detective Beck shares a wink with Ellie, and a half-second later, the gun explodes. Beck's blood and brain matter spray the crowd. Then, Beck's body slams the ground hard enough his head bounces. Ellie stands over Beck's body in a stupor as the police rush the scene. Digger places his arms around Ellie and tries to pry her away, but her body refuses. EMTs appear at her side and ask her to move away from Beck. Then a chair materializes for Ellie to sit. Her eyes are glassy, while her skin is pasty white. Ellie trembles.

Members of the task force surround Ellie as an EMT takes her vital signs. The EMT shows her vitals are typical, but he suggests a trip to the ER because of shock. Ellie hears him and refuses to go to the ER, and then the EMT hands her some wipes. Ellie looks at the EMT in bewilderment, not understanding the wipes. She looks down at her hands and notices blood covers her head to toe.

Watson leans into Ellie's ear and whispers, "it's not a bad idea to get checked out at the ER. You're in shock. Ellie, you know things happen when people come out of it."

Ellie looks up at the team, "I'm not leaving. I need to get cleaned up, and by the looks of it, several of us need a good cleaning too." She points at Digger and Rafter. Both sport blood on their clothes. "Here comes the crime scene unit. I'm sure they'll have questions. Once we answer those, we'll go to the hotel for a hot shower."

The crime scene unit takes charge of the aftermath along with police investigators, including Larkin. He separates the witnesses into segments, from closest to the incident to the farthest. Ellie is the number one witness, and Larkin joins Ellie's interview session. He doesn't want to leave her alone. Digger is with another detective answering questions.

Watson mentions to Bob about Kelly Knight being in the crowd. They know she goes nowhere in public with a chance of a story without a camera. While they questioned Watson, Bob found Kelly and asked her about the camera. Kelly admits she didn't ask her cameraman if he recorded the incident. She has seen nothing like that in her life. Kelly takes Bob's hand, and they walk to her van. Her cameraman sits at a video monitor when they open the door.

Kelly leans in, "Hey, Eddie, were you the recording when Beck fired the shot?"

Eddie grins, "I got the entire thing, Kelly." Just as he said it, Bob leaned his head in the door.

"The FBI needs the film, Eddie," Bob stated in his deep voice.

"Uh, okay. Can we keep a copy? We won't show it on the TV or anything. Just to prove I took it." Eddie asks.

"No copies, Eddie. This guy was a local police detective. We don't want the public watching it, but we appreciate you recording it for us. It will help in the investigation. Heck, I bet Agent Watson will give you an accommodation for your efforts." Bob glances at Kelly, pleading for her support.

Kelly struggles with the request but relinquishes the video. "Hand it over, Eddie. Outstanding work, though. I'll make sure the boss knows it too."

Bob leaves the van with a video of the incident. This will close the investigation as the video proves Detective Marshall Beck acted upon his own volition to commit suicide in public. Bob shivers when he thinks of the gravity of what's happened. It's sad to see people do this to themselves, but it's far worse to be the ones left behind.

Watson and Larkin huddle at the edge of the crime scene tape. They watch Bob saunter towards them. Bob hands Watson the video, "it's all here, Watson. From Beck's first bout of yelling to the gunshot. Eddie, Kelly's camera person, stayed with the scene until the crime scene unit and detectives arrived."

Larkin acknowledges Bob with a pat on the back. "Impressive job. Thanks for making this happen.

Saves the department a lot of personnel hours in the investigation."

Bob hands the video to Watson and says, "this is the only copy per Eddie. I have no way to confirm that statement."

With the video in hand, Watson marches to police headquarters. He wants to meet with the captain. It's time they release his task force from their interviews as they have answered questions for over an hour. He has proof no one was in cahoots with Beck.

After meeting the captain, Watson gathers his task force members off to the side and advises them they are free to go to the hotel. He requests no one to travel alone tonight and not to leave the hotel.

Everyone climbs into Bob's vehicle. He'll drive them to the hotel since Larkin must remain at the scene. No one mentions suicide even though all thoughts center on the afternoon incident.

Once out of the car, Digger brings up supper to the crowd. Everyone except Ellie agrees to meet in the hotel lounge at seven. Ellie skips dinner because she wants to rest. But Digger knows she's hurting, and she's trying to act strong. Ellie's face tells the truth. Her eyes are still glassy, with some color returning to her cheeks.

Digger gives her some space. After his shower and change of clothes, he walks into the lounge to meet the others. Rafter asks about Ellie. Digger shares his feelings about her hiding her true feelings about today's incident.

"You know, Digger, everyone handles stress differently. Maybe she just needs a little alone time to process it. After supper, she might be ready to talk. Otherwise, let her handle it in her way." Rafter offers.

After supper, the guys separate. This investigation exhausts everyone, as proven by the under-eye dark circles. Digger enters his room and notices Ellie shut the connecting door. He pulls it and realizes she locked it from her side. Tapping on the door, she doesn't respond, so he sends her a text message. No reply to that either. Digger prays Ellie is resting. He slides a note under the door expressing his love and turns in for the night.

Ellie can't bring herself to answer the door or text messages. She's not ready because the tears won't stop flowing. How could Marshall commit suicide holding her wrist? Why would he? This makes little sense to her. She's not ready to face anyone or answer any more questions. It seems every time she gets mixed up in one of Watson's investigations, something happens to her. During the last investigation in Montana, the killer stabbed her, and now this. Ellie wonders if she is bad luck.

Ellie dreams all night about the gunshot, and every time the gun fires, she wakes. She finally falls into a deep sleep around four in the morning, only awakened by Digger banging on the connecting door. Ellie drags herself to the door, "Digger, I'm here. What's so urgent?"

"We have another murder, and we wanted you to know in case you woke up and no one was around. I'll reach out when we return."

"Hold on, Digger. I'm coming with you. Give me ten minutes, and I'll meet you at the connecting door. I want you to walk with me." Ellie said in a soft voice.

"See you in ten," Digger replies, not sure how to react.

Ten minutes later, the lock on the connecting door turns. Digger waits on the other side. Ellie pulls her door open. Digger reaches in and pulls her into a hug. "I've been so worried about you being alone." He kisses her on the cheek.

"I'm not sure how I feel about the incident, but somehow I must push through it. I'm thinking about recertifying for a detective position at a police department. Watson's investigations are rough on me. I'm not sure if I'm the bad luck piece or what."

With raised eyebrows, Ellie shocked Digger with her revelations. "We need to talk about it. You can teach with me or be a consultant without seeing the scenes firsthand. Together, we can make this work. Come on. The guys are waiting."

The duo walks off the elevator to applause. Ellie shocks the group with her presence. "Stop it, guys. I just needed a little time to process it. I'm not sure

I'm over it, but I hear we have another murder scene."

Bob dangles the keys showing it is time to go. "This scene is not too far from here."

Digger glances at Ellie at every chance he gets. He needs to know she is mentally stable, and he doesn't feel that way. Ellie seems distant like thoughts crowd her head. Keeping a watch on her is Digger's primary concern. He refuses to lose her over a horrible incident. He might suggest her seeing a counselor. Someone that can help her process her emotions. Ellie is an independent lady, so he will need to approach the subject with a soft touch.

The scene is active when the group pulls into a lot of extended stay motels. Ellie catches Digger staring at her, and she winks at him. "Come on. Let's look at this one." Ellie is the first one out of the vehicle. The men trot to catch up to her. Ellie stops short when the putrid smell of blood hits her nostrils. She gasps as she gives her stomach time to settle.

Larkin walks over to the group, "this is bad, guys. The victim has been here for a few days without air conditioning. Grab a face mask, booties, and follow me."

After Larkin's description, Ellie wonders if she will make it through this one. The smell reminds her of Beck, but worse, much worse. Rigor has come and gone, and there is nothing but a limp body with signs of decomposition. With the rigor passing, he isn't sitting upright in the chair but slumped forward

171

and right. The bindings are the only things holding him in the chair.

Ellie starts her scene survey at the door, then left to right. This efficient apartment is tiny, so it is a quick visual tour. She places markers for the shooter's stand then she marks the blood smears. Ellie notices the shooter had less space to work with here. She asks one of the crime scene techs for a tape measure. She asks for help from her group to hold the tape measure at a precise spot on the floor. Carefully, she runs the tape until it satisfies her.

Watson walks in and watches the show. "What did you discover, Ellie?"

Ellie replies, "marker 20 is the shooter's stand, marker 21 is the blood smear which I think matches the other smears. That would suggest your shooter is six feet tall, give or take a little."

Digger looks at Ellie. "That's what you were measuring. Can you show me how you determined the height?"

"Sure. Since this area is smaller, it contains most of the blood. The shooter stands here." Ellie points out the area then says, "and fires in this direction. Look at the blood pattern. You can see his shape and then where the blood strikes the wall and cabinet. The other scenes were larger than this one, which makes determining the height of the shooter harder to see."

Larkin was the first to speak, "You have an eye for blood spatter. Just like Watson said."

"Thanks. Has anyone checked his chest for a carving?" Ellie inquires.

"I checked, but the body is in such terrible shape, the medical examiner will have to share the carving with us when he gets him on the table," Larkin explains. "It's so early in the day. We should have something by early afternoon."

"What do we know about the victim?" Digger asks.

Rafter speaks, "His name is LaShawn Josephs. African American. He turned eighteen three weeks ago. From what I can get from his co-worker, LaShawn was busted as part of a drive-by shooting. He was a passenger in the shooter's car. Oscar was his public defender, and he stayed at Terry's halfway house until a month ago. The victim worked at a carwash, and his co-workers stopped by to pick him up for work. He had been home for three days on a mini-vacation. The first time he's been off from work since he started. The owner gave him the time off as a birthday present."

"Some birthday present," Ellie says as she walks away.

"Digger, should she be working? If she needs to go home, then take her. I don't want to cause her more harm." Watson shares as Digger watches worry lines inch into his forehead.

"You need to discuss that with her. She says she's okay, but to me, she seems distant. Her face is pale and drawn."

The group agrees with Digger. Ellie climbs into the vehicle and reads an email when the men reach her. A grin forms on Ellie's face as she says, "Our Mrs. Teeter was adopted. I received confirmation from a genealogy site group. Now, I can try to track her through another site."

When the group walks into the conference room, breakfast is waiting. They stop at the doorway, "Is this for us, or did we walk in on someone else's meeting?" Rafter asks.

"This is for us," Watson explains. "Since the crime scene kept us from breakfast, I ordered some for us. Coffee and juice are on the back wall. Help yourself."

Everyone is ravenous, and they prove it by eating almost everything on the table. Watson loves to sit back and watch his teams interact with one another. He can tell a lot about his people by doing this, and this team seems closer than most. The last one in Montana was a complex group. With Bob tagging along, he is a pleaser. So, he helps merge different people into one cohesive group.

Ellie rolls her chair to a corner so she can pick up her study of Mrs. Teeter. Knowing the adoption angle is a big help. Ellie has a friend who helped her with another case find the adoptive parents. She'll contact her friend today.

The men peruse the worker's list from Chopper and Terry. They will interview workers over three or four days, starting with Chopper's house since he has the most. It would be nice to meet with his group today and tomorrow. Larkin makes the call to Chopper to arrange for the interviews. Chopper tries to brush Larkin off, but Larkin pushes back, and he agrees to let the interviews take place at the house.

Digger walks over to check on Ellie. She hasn't touched her computer for a while. He sees her wipe her eyes with a tissue as she stares at a picture as he approaches.

"Ellie." Digger whispers. "What are you looking at?"

"Hi, Digger. I'm trying not to break down. The tears come out of nowhere. This is a picture of the Scales of Justice. I wanted to see how many more deaths follow. Then I wonder what will happen if we don't catch the killer before the end?"

"You have too much going on in your head. Are you sure you want to stay in this investigation? The rest of the guys can finish it. We've done our part." Digger says as he waits on a reply.

"I can't leave in the middle of an investigation. Somehow, I'll make it through."

Digger walks over to Watson and shares his encounter with Ellie. "should I talk with her, Digger?"

"Leave her be, right now. Maybe later, you can mention leaving to her." The men hear movement in the room, and they watch as Ellie walks over to the board where they post the carvings. She takes a pen and begins numbering the carvings on her picture.

Ellie turns and faces the group, "it looks like a murder or two are missing. And we still have several to go before the picture is complete."

"Swell. Just what I need to hear." Watson adds.

"What's missing from the picture, Ellie?" Rafter questions

"A vertical line on the side of a chest. If this one occurred before the restaurant cook, it would have been a while back. That is worrisome. Where is this person, and why hasn't someone found them yet?" Ellie asks with a puzzled expression.

"You're correct, Ellie. With the map of murders, he could be anywhere. There is no rhyme or reason for the locations."

After Rafter's last statement, Ellie continues. She contemplated this question, but she's now ready to ask it. "Watson, have we considered the killer might target guys recently released from halfway houses?"

Chapter 15

All eyes grow wide as Ellie's revelation hits the group. "Interesting point, Ellie. If you had to guess, how recent would you consider?"

"I'm not sure. I was simply curious if it's a possibility. Since we've been concentrating on past cases, I just thought I'd ask."

Digger nods, "I like it. This could be it, Ellie. Where are the halfway house tenants lists for the last three months? Those will tell us the numbers released. Between the workers and the recent releases, we are gaining on this killer." A smile spreads across Digger's face as he surveys the room.

With the lists spread out on the table, Larkin notes Silas had eleven cases in the last three months, Tara had six, and Oscar sits in the middle at seven. Rafter shares his idea of narrowing the cases to those guys with dirty blond hair, which matches our description. "If these don't pan out, we can add more to our interviews."

Larkin agrees and says, "let's meet the guys in the defender's office. Silas will be the first. Three guys, Titus, Jerry, and Calon, match the description. Since the records don't list height, we can rule the guys out once we see them."

"I'll call Silas and set up the interviews for this afternoon unless he's in court," Rafter says, then adds. "Digger, we received three calls last night from the tip line, which need further attention. Are you handling those, or would you rather I pass them along to the patrol officers?"

"While you're setting the interview appointments, I'll return the calls for the skulls."

Digger walks to another office and sits behind an empty desk with his messages. He grabs the first one and dials. On the fifth ring, a gruff-sounding man answers. Digger identifies himself and begins with questions about the skulls. The man's tone softens as he discusses the skulls with Digger. He admits to not knowing their names, but they visited his old neighborhood often. The lady is Mrs. Teeter's mother. They lived south as in, not Pennsylvania. This caller lived two houses down from the Teeter's and wondered what happened to them. Another neighbor stated the Teeter's moved to help a sick relative. The caller assumed it was Mrs. Teeter's mother.

All the while, the caller spoke, Digger jots notes. His mind races ahead about this information. How can they find Mrs. Teeter's parents without a name? Ellie's genealogy site could provide the information.

Digger calls the next message in line. A young guy answers the phone and stammers when Digger identifies himself. The guy says he has seen them around town but knows nothing else and hangs up. An uneasy feeling creeps into Digger's soul. He calls the number back, and its routed to voice mail. The voice mail is the typical robot voice saying the phone owner is not available. Digger sends a text message too.

The third message was from a lady who enjoyed talking. She never said much about the skulls, but she kept Digger on the phone for thirty minutes, just rambling. He discovered the caller lives east of the city, so at least that part was right. She offered no help to identify the skulls. She is a lonely lady looking for companionship.

Ellie is on her phone in the conference room, as is Watson, while Larkin stares at the murder board. "Digger, they murdered the victims before their cases made it to trial and shortly after their release from the halfway house. The killer is familiar with halfway houses. Either by currently living in one or in the past or as a worker. I'm leaning toward the first one."

Rafter joins the men at the board, "Silas agrees to let us interview the three guys from his list in his office. None of them strike him as a murderer, but then again, he doesn't know them. They try to make a good impression with him since he represents them in a criminal case. He's calling them now."

After lunch, Silas calls Rafter and explains that he set the afternoon appointments, beginning at three. The group meets to discuss interview questions. Each guy will receive the same questions, so they have a means of comparison. If any of the guys seems agitated or not truthful, they will get a second interview at police headquarters.

At three sharp, the group joins Silas in his conference room. Calon is the first guy to show, and his hair is dirty blond, shorter than six feet, but not much. He is wearing blue jeans with a plain t-shirt. The police arrested Calon with drugs, enough to be labeled a distributor. This is the second offense and his first time assigned to Silas. Calon stays at a halfway house on the other side of town. He tried to get into Terry's or Chopper's house, but they were full. He says he understands the consequences of hanging with the wrong crowd. His release date is next Friday.

Calon left the room, and the group glanced at each other. "He seems like a normal kid with nothing to hide. I would rule him out as a killer." Larkin comments, "but he could become a victim." Then he tilts his head when he glimpses Digger.

Titus enters next with a swagger. He confirms his arrest record of drugs, theft, robbery, and the list continues. He also has dirty blond hair, with dirty being the appropriate word. It smells as if Titus doesn't like baths. He makes eye contact with everyone around the table. Titus is playing a bad guy with his attitude while briefly answering the questions. His answers are what we want to hear. Ellie notices his eyes turn up and to the right. The sure sign of a lie. Titus confirms he stays at Chopper's, and he helps around the house when not working. Silas reminds Titus his release date starts in ten days. The group watches as his eyes grow big as if surprised by the announcement.

As soon as Titus leaves, the group converges on Silas. "What do you know about this guy, Silas?" Larkin prods.

Silas opens his file and produces Titus' arrest and case records. "This is it. All we receive in our assignments are the offender's arrest record and a prior assignment. We meet with the person and go from there. I know nothing about his background unless he is a repeat offender. Titus is a repeat. He stayed with Chopper in the past for the same reasons. This is his last chance with Chopper or any halfway house."

"I thought halfway houses were a step to rehabilitation, not somewhere you go in and out." Digger mentions.

"They are. However, there are a few of our offenders that receive multiple chances at these houses. Chopper is notorious for taking guys a second or third time. He hates to give up on a kid." Silas explains.

Silas looks up at the doorway, "come on in, Jerry."

Jerry looks around the room at the group of people. "What's this, Silas? Am I in trouble?"

Larkin stands and introduces everyone. Ellie noted Jerry's reluctance to enter the room with the number of people around the table. Jerry sits and wipes his hands on his pants leg.

Digger starts with the questions. Jerry answers and becomes more relaxed as his shoulders settle. His record starts back as a juvenile with theft, and then as a young adult, he gravitated to more serious crime. His arrest record lists robbery with multiple counts. Jerry explains he tried to get enough money to buy his mom a birthday present. He admits it was stupid. Silas was a great public defender, and he worked hard to get him a lesser sentence. He was in prison for a year, out in eight months, and has been in a halfway house for three months. His release date is in thirty days, and Jerry is ready for the outside world. He'll never go back to prison.

Ellie marks his name off of the list even though he is six feet tall. Jerry is too eager for the outside to be a murderer. Murder is something you cannot walk away from with time served. "Who is next on our list? Titus is the only one I question so far."

"No one else is on the list for today. Tara scheduled her guy, Paul, for nine in the morning since he works the night shift. He will come straight from work. Oscar has guys for tomorrow afternoon." Rafter explains.

Digger reviews his phone call with the young guy. This guy concerns him. "Hey, Rafter, can someone ping a phone for me?" Digger explains his conversation with the caller and how the caller is not answering his phone now.

"Sure, Digger. Give me the number, and I'll make the request." Digger hands Rafter a sticky note with the number on it. Rafter states, "Be back in a second."

While Rafter is away, Digger ponders his next move with the skulls. He wants Kelly to contact a national station and broadcast the story there. The other calls to the tip line have been useless. Second-guessing himself, Digger wonders if he should not have aged the couple. Maybe someone would have recognized them without the age enhancement.

Rafter enters the room with a look of doom on his face. "Sorry, Digger, but the phone is off, and the battery removed. It is also a burner phone. So, the owner may not use it again. I've left the number with the tech guys, and they'll check it periodically the next several days."

"Thanks, Rafter. I'll take whatever help I can get. The caller sounded as if they know more than they shared." Digger adds.

After a long day, the group spends a quiet night at the hotel. Ellie's concern lies with those guys scheduled to leave the halfway house in the next few days. She doesn't want to see them as a victim of their killer. Ellie pulls out her notebook and doodles because her mind works while her hands move. How does the killer know when someone is released from a halfway house? The task force must catch the killer before he strikes again.

The following morning, Tara sits behind an ornate desk sipping coffee from a mug with the Scales of Justice printed outside. Digger pauses entry when he sees the cup, unsure how to react to the visual. Ellie and Larkin notice the mug, too, as their eyes pass over Digger's.

"Good morning. We are moving down the hall to the conference room." Tara stands and waves her arm toward the door.

Larkin takes the lead, "good morning, Tara. Have you confirmed Paul's appointment time?"

"We spoke late yesterday afternoon, and he agreed to meet this morning. He's one of my punctual ones, so I'm not worried about him showing."

Tara leads the group into the conference room, and each slips into a chair. Paul's appointment is at 9:00 am, and the group stares at the walls waiting for his arrival. Tara trots to her office and checks with the receptionist. Tara's brows furrow while sending a text message to Paul's phone. This is unlike him. He has never been a no-show for their appointments.

Thirty minutes after the text and one hour after the appointment, the group leaves Tara's office. She provides Larkin with Paul's cell phone number and gives directions to his halfway house. "We haven't stopped at Paul's house. If I remember, it's a smaller one."

Ellie pulls up the picture online of the halfway house. "It's a gorgeous older home converted into a halfway house. I can't wait to see the inside."

A short ride over, and they park in the adjacent lot. Three vehicles park facing the house. Larkin scribbles the tag numbers in his book. A nifty detective trick he picked up many years ago from his mentor. An older man with rigid lines on his face and stringy gray hair sits in a rocker on the wide front porch. Larkin introduces the group, and the man stands and shakes hands with everyone. Hank ushers the group inside to the kitchen table.

Ellie takes it all in as she strolls along the foyer. The hardwood floor glistens in the soft light from the chandeliers hanging from the twenty-foot high ceiling. Crown molding surrounds the ceiling with its thick wood carved into intricate designs and painted glossy champagne. "This is the house I would love to live in," Ellie exclaims.

"Until you are stuck with the air conditioning or heat bill. I don't care how much time and effort you put in plugging holes from the outside. You always miss some. But thank you for the compliment. This house is special." Hank shares Ellie's love of the place.

After everyone sits, Hank starts the conversation, "I know you came by to check out my house. Who are you looking for, and why?"

"Paul missed our appointment this morning at Tara's office. Tara expressed how punctual Paul is, and it concerns us. Is Paul here?" Larkin inquires.

"He isn't here. Paul works nights. He mentioned your meeting to me, so I assumed he was heading to Tara's after work. Let me call his boss." Hank steps away from the table and walks into a sunroom off the kitchen. The sunroom faces a small backyard. The fenced yard has a walking path, birdbath, and several swings. Tucked into a corner of the backyard sits a gazebo with built-in benches.

Hank comes over to the table and sits with a sigh. "Paul isn't at work. His boss knew of the meeting this morning, and Paul left work on time. I'm concerned now. This isn't like him. He goes to work and is back here for breakfast. Where else could he be?" Hank's face shows worry as he wipes his hand down his face then through his hair.

Ellie suggests Rafter ping his phone as it will help narrow the focus. While Larkin works with Rafter, Digger and Ellie, ask Hank for a house tour. He obliges, and they begin in the sunroom. Hank shares this is his favorite room. He uses it for reading and thinking. On the other side of the sunroom is the formal dining room. The table is massive, seating twelve easily.

Hank talks for the next fifteen minutes about the house and how some of his tenants helped him revive the old place. Ellie asks about Hank's story because she knows he has one. He went to prison for manslaughter after being labeled a habitual violator with multiple driving under the influence arrests. Hank traveled home from a long night at the bar when he swerved his car, and it jumped a curb, striking a pedestrian. The pedestrian died on impact, and the rest is history.

Digger adds, "well, you made the best of an unpleasant situation. You have a great place here, Hank. Thanks for helping us out."

"Rafter called back. Nothing on Paul's phone." Larkin addresses us with a scowl on his face.

Hank looks at Larkin, "Are you saying the phone is off? Paul never turns his off. He uses it for an alarm too. Let's visit his room. I haven't shown you that yet."

Hank led the way and opened the door to Paul's room. The bed is made, and there isn't a speck of dust. Hank opens the closet door, and Paul's duffle bag is still on the shelf. "if he travels, this bag goes everywhere with him. It doesn't appear Paul had any intention of leaving."

"What kind of vehicle does Paul drive?" Digger inquires.

"He has an older model gray pickup truck. The kid saved more money than anyone I've had come through here. He refused to put it on a newer vehicle because of his job. Paul didn't want a new vehicle sitting on the side of a highway while he poured asphalt. I didn't check the lot. Let's go out back."

The group follows Hank out the back of the house through a few turns. Paul's truck is missing too. "Hank, do you have the license plate number for Paul's truck?"

"No, I don't. Most of my guys can never afford a vehicle, so I didn't bother asking."

Larkin pacifies Hank, "no worries. I'll have one of my guys dig it out from the DMV."

Rafter places a BOLO on Paul's truck after his conversation with Larkin. Both men feel foul play is involved. Paul is notoriously punctual and has saved a lot of money for his release date. This doesn't sound like someone who has plans to run away. The confusing issue is Paul goes nowhere other than work and the halfway house. Both places are in the dark.

With nothing left to do at the house, the group expresses their efforts in locating Paul, and Hank will keep in touch. Once the group closes the car doors, Ellie says, "I don't like this. It seems a little too convenient for me."

"I agree with Ellie. But what I don't understand is if the killer took Paul, he changed his tactics. The halfway house released the earlier victims, and they lived in their own place. Why change now?" Digger ponders. "Where would the killer do the deed if Paul lived at a halfway house? The residents of the house would hear the murder or at least smell it."

Larkin rubs his chin as he considers the options. He looks around the street where the halfway house sits. Other homes and commercial businesses border the house. Some of the converted houses are now attorney offices, day spas, and the list goes on. If he wasn't taken from here, he was at Tara's.

Chapter 16

The vehicle revs as Larkin throws the vehicle in reverse and pushes the pedal. "Someone took Paul from the public defenders parking lot. That's the only other place he was going today."

"Rafter, Larkin. Have a patrol unit meet us in the parking lot of Tara Jiff's office. I'm betting Paul's vehicle is there. If it is, I'll call for a crime scene unit."

In a quivering voice, Ellie whispers, "Oh no. You mean we left Tara's office, and Paul's vehicle was there the whole time we've been with Hank."

Digger reaches over and takes Ellie's hand. "We know nothing has happened to Paul. Let's take one step at a time." Ellie glances at Digger and shakes her head.

"You know Paul is in danger, just like I do. Please don't patronize me. I won't break." Ellie stated as she removed her hand from Digger's grasp and looked out the side window. The front seat guys made sure their heads faced forward. After the back seat interaction, they didn't want to be a part of the conversation.

With Larkin speeding, the lot appears sooner than they expected. Tires squeal as Larkin maneuvers the vehicle into the lot. They scoped out two parking lanes when a patrol officer called for Larkin. He has Paul's car in the next section.

The group parks behind the patrol car and exits their vehicle while staring at Paul's. With guns drawn, Larkin and the officer approach Paul's truck. They slide along the car until they reach the windows. The cab and truck bed are empty. Paul locked the vehicle upon his arrival, and it appears untouched. Larkin called the courthouse where the public defenders work and requested video footage of today's front door entries.

Digger called Tara and asked her if Paul contacted her in their absence. Paul has not reached her, and she asked for an update on our investigation. Digger shares what he can with her.

When Larkin and Digger end their calls, the group gathers at the vehicle to determine their next step. Bob asks the group, "Do you think the killer kidnapped Paul from the parking lot? Is that why we are here? I've reviewed the case notes, and there is nothing to indicate kidnapping from the killer. So, why would he change his tactic now?"

Ellie explains, "sometimes killers will change their mode to confuse the authorities."

Bob nods as if he understands the possible changes. "So, we consider the kidnapping to have happened here. We need eyes on the lot. Are there cameras in this area of the lot?"

Digger tilts his head up and twirls as he seeks to find cameras. "One there and there, and another one back there, but tree limbs might obscure that one."

"Add the parking lot cameras to my request," Larkin adds.

All eyes turn on Larkin. "Oscar's first appointment is in thirty minutes. Let's scour the lot and see if Paul reappears, and with our presence, maybe the killer will leave Paul alone."

Everyone meanders around the lot, looking for anything out of the ordinary. Cars enter and exit the lot every few seconds. A courthouse is a busy place. People stare at us as they walk to their vehicles since they are unaccustomed to people wandering the lot.

Twenty-five minutes later, Larkin gathers us to walk to Oscar's office. As we enter, Oscar meets with a young guy, and no one sits in the lobby. So we spread out and took up most of the lobby chairs. Once Oscar finishes, he escorts the young guy out the door and turns to face us.

"I heard about Paul. Have you found him?" Oscar inquires.

Larkin stands and addresses Oscar, "No, we haven't found him. We searched the area and found his truck. It looks like he made it here but then vanished."

"Keep me updated, will you? Ron is two minutes late. Should I be nervous?"

"Hey, Oscar. What's going on?" Ron stands in the doorway with a strange expression on his face. By the look, he can't decide whether to run or stay.

"Ron, I am glad to see you. Come on in. These people have a few questions for you."

The group enters a small side conference room. It's a tight fit for the group, but once everyone squeezes into the chairs, Oscar introduces the group then Larkin takes the lead. Ron faces the group, and his face shows astonishment. There is no way he is a killer as his face gives away his feelings with every question. Ron and Paul are acquaintances from their past. Their work is similar as they are both in construction. Ron is unfamiliar with Paul's patterns and friends.

Toward the end of Ron's meeting, Larkin narrows the reasons for this visit. Ron explains he's not a killer. Life is going right for him as he'll move from Hank's into an apartment within four weeks. He has completed his court-mandated requirements for release. He plans to return to Hank's house to help as a mentor.

Ron's statement triggers a thought in Bob's head. "How often do halfway house residents come back to help at their halfway house?"

"I'm not sure. A few of the houses have return residents mentor the new residents or those having trouble adjusting to re-entry into the real world, and some returns work at multiple houses through the county."

Zachary, our next visitor, sits slumped in a chair in the lobby when Ron leaves. Ron and Zachary do not speak as they pass each other. Oscar points to our room, and he follows Zachary toward the door. At the doorway, Zachary stops before entering the room when he realizes its full. "What's this, Oscar?"

Oscar introduces the group and explains the circumstances of the meeting. Zachary is skeptical of police or any law enforcement. He fidgets with a ring while answering questions. His release date is seven weeks away, and he states he has a place to go and a good job. He is a manager at a fast-food place and has had two pay increases. Zachary does not know Paul.

Once the meeting ends and Zachary is out of earshot, Digger says, "our killer is a resident or a mentor, no doubt about it. We need a list of mentors to rule them out. If Ron is right, there aren't many. We could handle those in two days. Then, our concentration can shift to residents only."

Ellie disagrees with a nod, "I don't believe our killer is a mentor. He is a resident and one nearing his release date."

The other men glance from Digger to Ellie and back. Larkin swallows and tries to please both parties. "What about splitting duties with Digger working the mentors, and Ellie takes the residents?"

No one answers Larkin at first, then Digger relinquishes. "I'm good with Ellie's suggestion. She is more of a profiler than I." After the statement, he turns and walks out of the office. The others follow him.

Oscar calls after them, "Don't forget to send updates." He steps away and shakes his head, not understanding the relationship chemistry.

Everyone slips into the car without a spoken word. Larkin drives to headquarters, and as he turns into the lot, the courthouse tech unit calls with a report on the cameras. He slams his fist on the steering wheel and returns to the courthouse. Larkin's face is red, and he chews on his inner cheek as he drives.

Ellie addresses the group. "I apologize for my remarks, but I don't enjoy wasting time, and the mentors will be a waste of time. Once a resident becomes a mentor, he would have no reason to kill people. His statement is the Scales of Justice. The killer is unhappy with the result of his case or the public defender."

"No apologies necessary. Everyone has opinions, and all avenues need investigating." Larkin offers. "My hope is the video feed shows us the killer. Then, we can find him and end his run."

The group follows Larkin into the security office at the courthouse. The head of security has the video cued. Once everyone sits, the video begins. They watch four views of the parking lot. Not one camera shows a front facial aspect of the kidnapper. The assumption is Paul knows this guy. Paul walked away from the lot and out of the camera range of his own free will. The kidnapper wore a cap pulled low over his brow, a baggy shirt, and low-hanging baggy pants.

Ellie mentions the bloody smear marks from murder scenes. "Those smears could result from pants dragging through the blood. If that is so, the killer's pants would have a trace amount of blood on them even if he washed the pants."

"Interesting fact, Ellie. Next time we visit a halfway house, we need to pay attention to the guys wearing long pants touching the floor." Bob ponders this information. "Does anyone remember seeing a guy where his pants dragged the floor?"

"I'm not sure I paid close enough attention to the guys since I concentrated on the dirty blond hair and their attitude. I propose we look at all the residents with matching descriptions. Even though we are uncertain, the guy in the description is our killer. We are taking a chance on that too." Digger suggests.

"I agree with Digger. We can start with the description we have and then branch out if we need to. Also, Larkin, can we get the public to help in locating Paul?" Bob added.

"Watson might let Kelly run with Paul's disappearance. I'll speak to him before we move forward. I suggest we speak with all halfway house residents who match our description. Six guys on our current list, with one of those missing. That is not boding well for an acceptable outcome." Larkin analyzes their situation. His phone rings as he contemplates his next step. Hank calls, expressing concern for Paul's safety, and asks if he must file a missing person report. Larkin glances around before asking Hank to hold off on the report because he works on something with the media.

"I'm sure you heard the conversation. Hank wants to report Paul as a missing person. We should handle the report for him. We'll meet with Watson at headquarters."

Watson waits for the group in the conference room as they enter. The mood turns somber when Watson addresses them. "What happened this morning? We have a missing person."

Larkin stands at the murder board and adds new intel as the conversation progresses. Paul is most vital as they have no guesses on his location. They checked again with work, and Hank called advising Paul hadn't called or returned home. After discussing Paul, Larkin moved on to their meeting with Titus, Jerry, Calon, Ron, and Zachary. Other tidbits from the conference include Titus not being ready to leave the house, Jerry, Calon, Ron, and Zachary having law enforcement phobia.

Ellie expresses concern about the likelihood of these guys becoming victims since their release is within a few days or weeks. She asks about the possibility of police protection.

Watson didn't approve individual police protection but agrees to have extra patrols when these guys move out of their homes. We'll need to compile a list of release dates to have the patrol units ready. He requests a picture of Paul and says he'll call Kelly for help in locating him.

Digger receives a text message from Rafter asking him to come to his desk for a message from the tip line. Digger excuses himself and walks downstairs to see Rafter.

Rafter holds up a message, and by the grin on his face, he is eager to share it. "This is good, Digger. The caller is from Marion County, West Virginia. He says he knew these people a long time ago. Digger grabs the note and trots back upstairs. He slips into an empty office and dials the number.

The older man answers on the second ring and doesn't hesitate to jump into a tirade on the skulls. He explains he was eating a TV dinner when this pretty reporter showed up with a couple of headshots. The caller recognizes the man's face as a co-worker from many years ago. If he recalls, the man's last name is Anderson, but he can't remember the first name. The caller always wondered what happened to the guy. Digger slides in a question about where the man might have lived at the time. The caller said he lived in a duplex down the street from him. Digger thanked the older man, and the call ended.

Armed with additional information, Digger sets out to find Ellie. "Ellie, I have additional information on the skulls. An older man from Marion County, West Virginia, called the tip line. The man's last name is Anderson. However, the caller can't remember his first name. He had no recollection of the female. Do we have enough information to help identify the man?"

"Yes. I'll enter the search criteria for West Virginia right now." As Ellie opens her laptop, she peeks up at Digger. She admits she loves him, but can she live with him? Over the last few days, this question has resonated. After Beck's suicide, decisions are not coming easy for her. With Digger by her side, she thought she could handle the emotional toll, but now, she is unsure.

"I entered the query, Digger. Now, we wait. I hope this name works on identification. At least we would conclude half of our investigation." Ellie said as she lowered her head and rubbed her hands on her pants.

"Ellie, you would tell me if something were wrong, right? I can get you back home if that's what it takes." Digger rubs her shoulder and feels the knots under her sweater. "You have knots in your shoulders. Let me give them a rubdown. Somehow you need to relax." Digger steps behind Ellie and massages the tension knots in her shoulders and neck. After a few minutes, Digger feels the tension subside, and Ellie relaxes.

"Thanks for the massage. I might have you give me another one before bed. It might help me sleep. When I lay in bed, my mind continues." Ellie explains.

Watson walks in as Digger moves away from Ellie. "I have a dinner date with Kelly. I'll ask her to help locate Paul. Bob will drop you at the hotel. Larkin and his captain are meeting, so you two have a night alone. See you in the morning at eight for breakfast."

Digger lifts his right eyebrow, "did he say we have tonight alone? Because if he did, you would see me jump for joy. Let's go, Ellie. The night moves way too fast when you enjoy yourself."

The duo enjoys dinner alone in the hotel lounge. Ellie shares her feelings about the investigation and Beck. She accepts his death now and doesn't blame herself even though she wants to know the reason behind his death. No one in the department will talk to her about it, and she questions if they are trying to protect her from the reason. Digger suggests she speak with Watson. If anyone can help, he can.

While the twosome sits at dinner, Watson picks Kelly up at her place. He inhales when he sees her. She dresses to perfection from head to toe. He guides her to the vehicle and then wipes the sweat from his brow. He chastises himself for acting like a school kid around her. They share childhood stories, and then the questions start about past romances. Kelly had a failed marriage and no children, while Watson never made it to marriage. Although he was engaged once, that tidbit is unknown because his fiancé was killed in a drive-by when the bullet was meant for him. He was a homicide detective working a gang murder, and the members wanted to chase Watson away by putting a bullet in him, but his fiancé stepped in front of the bullet. She died on the concrete sidewalk outside of their townhouse. Eight months later, he started his FBI career tracking serial killers.

Watson leans back in his chair and studies Kelly. He admits to himself he likes her more and more. Could they make it in a relationship? How can an FBI agent and a reporter make it work? They could share nothing about their work life. A somber mood washes over Watson as the realization hits that he and Kelly could never make a couple.

Kelly notices the change in Watson, "What's wrong, Watson? Did I offend you?" Her forehead creases with worry lines as she waits for his response.

"Not at all. Just a lot on my mind. I need to ask you for help again but don't think I invited you to dinner for the help. The dinner is for us. I wanted to spend time with you outside of the police headquarters."

"I'm glad you did because I like you, Watson. We understand each other, and that's hard to find. Now, what can I help you with?" Kelly reaches across the table and holds Watson's hand while her thumb moves back and forth across the top.

Watson looks at their hands and forgets her question. He blushes, "What was your question again?"

"You said you need my help. What is it, Watson?"

With his composure restored, Watson explains Paul's situation. He asks Kelly to run a story on him, asking for anyone with information on his whereabouts to contact police headquarters. Watson tells Kelly about the parking lot cameras, the halfway house, and the public defender's role as he spills the entire investigation to her.

After he finishes, Kelly takes a sip of tea and says, "you realize you gave me your entire case, right? I'll keep the other information out of the story and concentrate on Paul, but I want the exclusive when this is over."

Since her hand is still resting on his, he turns his wrist and shakes her hand. They both giggle. The night ends, and Watson drops her at her doorstep. He might consider trying a relationship with her after all.

Chapter 17

The following day the elevator deposits the duo in the hotel lobby. Digger and Ellie glance around but not finding another member of the team. They walk into the breakfast area. Just as Ellie pours coffee, Watson appears in a flush. "We got another one. Get your coffee to go. Larkin is already at the scene, and Bob has our vehicle ready at the door."

"Another one already. The picture is almost complete. What will he do after he finishes? Will he continue on his current path?" Digger shakes his head in bewilderment.

"More than likely, he'll find another picture or a different way to express his displeasure in our justice system. What upsets me is we can't determine if he's a current resident at one of our halfway houses or if he's already on the outside? Our team might interview more than we originally thought."

Bob stands next to the driver's door, waiting for the group to arrive. He gives a slight nod as a morning hello since the morning starts with a murder. No one likes to start their day at a murder scene.

Once the riders are situated, Digger asks Watson for any information they have on this murder. The victim's name is Jose Diaz, early twenties, and he works on a landscaping crew. His crew stopped to pick him up from his two-bedroom home on the way to the job site, and when they got no answer, they called the police for a welfare check. A rookie patrol officer found him and called Rafter. Rafter notified Larkin.

Watson answers his phone and murmurs to the caller. Ellie peeks at Digger as they try to determine the caller. Digger decides Kelly called Watson. So, their night must have been exciting, or she is helping locate Paul, and she has a follow-up question.

Watson shares, "Kelly's afternoon and evening broadcast will spotlight our search for Paul. I have provided her with an updated photo of Paul. If there is any additional information on Paul, let me know so I can pass it along. We are labeling him as a person of interest, not a victim."

Unmarked and marked law enforcement vehicles litter the driveway and curb in front of the Diaz house. A landscaping truck sits across the street with a crew staring at the home. The crew is easily visible as they wear fluorescent yellow t-shirts.

Ellie stops at the door, turns, and surveys the area. The officer guarding the entrance opens it for Ellie and her team. The smell knocks her for a loop every time. She kicks herself for not being able to handle it, but she pushes forward. Jose lived in a small but neat home except for the blood. It's everywhere. It appears a struggle occurred here, and if it did, this is a first.

Blood covers the kitchen floor, cabinets, and ceiling. There are several smeared fingerprints on the kitchen counter as if the killer laid his weapon down. Ellie's eyebrows bunch together, and she wrings her hands while examining the scene. Silas's business card rest under a magnet on the refrigerator door. Ellie makes a note of this as she points it out to the team.

Next, she walks into the family room, and there sits the leader of the landscaping crew. He is visibly upset with unshed tears waiting for the wave to burst. The leader speaks low, so it is hard for Ellie to listen, but she heard he was released from Chopper's house a few weeks ago. Chopper noticed how good Jose was in his yard and suggested Jose join his team. Jose fell right in step with the crew like he had been there forever.

Digger asks Larkin about the carving. Larkin says, "follow me."

They walk up to the deceased guy, and Larkin takes a glove and gently lifts the guy's shirt. The carving is there. It's a diagonal straight line on the left side of the chest. The top starts towards the center, and it falls outward from there towards the rib area.

After they inspect the carving, Digger joins Ellie, and they discuss the scene amongst themselves. "Do you see what I see, Digger?" Ellie asks.

"Are you referring to a struggle and a messy scene? If so, yes. This scene is far different from the others. Did Jose put up a fight?"

"Jose is not a big guy, but he appears well built. If the killer had trouble subduing Jose, that information would help us narrow our focus. After looking at the fingerprints, our killer wears latex gloves when he commits the crime. There were no print lines in the blood on the counter. The shooter's standing place was harder to discern this time because of the blood spatter. My thought is Jose was bleeding before the gunshot." Ellie points to the victim. "And possibly the killer's DNA is in here somewhere."

Digger adds to the information, "Jose was a resident at Chopper's and assigned to Silas. My fear is the killer will try to kill Silas and or Chopper. When Larkin finishes up with the crime scene unit, we need to share our theory."

The duo exits the home and heads back to the vehicle. Bob sits in the driver's seat with the door open, and he leans against the door frame. His phone touches his ear as he listens to someone. Every so often, Bob grunts an acknowledgment to the caller.

Ellie and Digger stand slightly outside of earshot. They didn't want to intrude if Bob's call was top secret. They continue their discussion of the scene. "What about our victims' living arrangements? Do they live alone, or does the killer know when to visit? We've had no word of a second person being in any of the homes at the time of the murder." Digger points out.

With a notebook in hand, Ellie refers to it as she reviews the other murder scenes. "I can't confirm two scenes. The others I have noted the victim's lived alone. Once we get back to headquarters, I can verify the living arrangements with the murder book. However, I suspect all the victims lived alone, but how does the killer know this information?"

Digger calls Silas and informs him of Jose's death. Silas is speechless until Digger mentions Chopper. He confirms Jose stayed with Chopper and did a remarkable job on the lawn. Silas asks over and over, "Who is doing this and why? The killer is lucky he spent time at a halfway house. He got out of prison early as part of a transition period. Other inmates are not that lucky."

"When we catch him, we'll ask him for you, Silas. Your safety concerns us with your connections to the victims. Would you reconsider police protection?"

"No. I don't want to spend taxpayer money protecting an older man like me. Do what you can to find this killer. Thanks for calling." Digger and Ellie share a look of sadness.

The duo slides into their seats when Bob waves them over. "Kelly called Watson asking if Paul has any family members in town. She wants to interview them before her broadcast. Do either of you know?"

"Hank might know. I don't remember asking him in our interview." Digger offers.

"Can you place a call to Hank for me, Digger?" Bob pleads.

On the ride back to headquarters, Digger speaks with Hank, and without a pause, Hank advises Paul to share nothing about his past or his family. His house requirements do not include asking family members contact information. Most of the offenders list their house manager or another offender as an emergency contact.

Digger conveys the conversation to Bob, who looks dejected. "Nothing about this investigation has been easy. I'm without a reason for it to be this way." Bob says more to himself than the group. However, they nod their heads in agreement without commenting.

Larkin brings up the rear as everyone enters the conference room. "Take a seat, everyone. First off, the order of business is Chopper. We need to call him about Jose. I'll call on speakerphone, and if you have a question, jump in."

Chopper answers on the first ring. Larkin identifies himself and admits to being on speakerphone with the group. Chopper expresses a myriad of emotions. He starts off the conversation by saying how upset he is about these murders. Then he asks the group if his house is being targeted. No one can answer since other halfway houses are missing residents too.

A break in the conversation allows Ellie to ask about Jose. Chopper sniffs then starts. Jose was a little standoffish to the guys when he first arrived. However, he became friends with Titus and another offender, Calon. I think that's his name. He lives at

Hanks's house on the other side of town. Jose and Calon met on a job if I remember. Jose worked on a landscaping crew, and he helped around Chopper's house. Chopper shares his admiration for Jose's landscape design ability, and he mentioned to Jose many times about him helping Jose start his own business.

Ellie's unshed tears sit at the brink of falling over as she listens to Chopper describe Jose. She can see Chopper sitting in his favorite chair on the porch overlooking Jose's work. It is heartbreaking to listen to Chopper.

After Chopper's call, the group takes a break and composes themselves. This case is taking a toll on the lot. Ellie isn't the only person with emotions. Every day it gets harder and harder to hold the feelings in check.

Kelly's broadcast made the mid-day news. The group watches the television as she presents a missing person plea. Paul's picture covers the screen with the tip line printed on the bottom. She doesn't elaborate on the police involvement because they want to know his whereabouts. The newscast was short, but Kelly put emphasis on missing and presumed to be in grave danger.

Meanwhile, Bob explains the requested traffic cam videos from around the courthouse. The cams show Paul and another person about the same height walking away from the courthouse. The next camera in line malfunctioned, and the cross-street cameras show no visual of Paul.

Bob shows the videos to the group and adds the direction of travel is west. Paul walks side by side with someone with no visible weapons. Paul glances back over his shoulder as if asking a question to his friend. The other guy never breaks his stride as he continues walking without looking back.

With a map on the wall, the group considers where the duo might travel next. Chopper's, Terry's, and Hank's houses are in the general area. However, they are miles apart. Digger is the first one to announce Paul's friend had a vehicle stashed somewhere. There is no reason to walk to one of the known halfway houses when Paul had a vehicle at the courthouse. So, where did they go?

Since the cameras provided no definitive answers, Watson urges the group to leave the cameras and work with the halfway house residents. He emphasized multiple houses, and he instructed the team to keep the description in the back of their mind and interview all residents. Then, in a demanding tone, Watson states they should not have strayed from their original plan, and the description might have thrown the investigation off in the wrong direction.

The group takes its marching orders in stride. Someone is getting under Watson's skin. His nature is calm, but today, something bothers Watson. With his eyebrows bunched up, he rubs his hand across the back of his neck while reviewing a report. After he peruses the information, he lifts his head and faces the group.

"The DNA results are in from Jose's scene. First, we need to thank the Crime Scene Unit for expediting the results. We have two people who lost blood at the scene. Most belonged to Jose, but the crime scene tech found a tiny drop of blood belonging to another party. They are working on separating the blood now. The tech is not sure the blood drop will be enough for a DNA match. Just know, if the killer suffered an injury in the struggle with Jose, he might lie low for a while. This might play in our favor."

Watson retreats to the snack bar for coffee. On his return trip, his phone rings. Kelly calls to check on him, and his mood makes a one-hundred-and-eighty-degree turn. When he enters the room, he smiles, and Ellie winks at him, then he blushes. Upon realizing that Kelly makes him feel good, he slips back out into the hallway to chat.

Ellie asks a question of the group, "Which halfway house has lost the most residents since the murder spree began?"

"Good question." Larkin points out.

Digger searches for the notes with the tabulations. He flips pages and adds tick marks to his list. "So far, I show Silas was the public defender on seven murders, Oscar three, and is Tara at two. Chopper has lost six prior residents, Terry with four and Hank with two. Based on these numbers, Silas and Chopper have the most contact with the residents. Unless someone calls the halfway houses once a past resident has died, they have no way to know unless they watch it on the news."

Bob glances at the room, "No wonder it concerns Chopper. If someone murdered six of my prior residents, it would scare me too. But, since it involved other houses, I don't see the killer targeting one house over another. Do you all agree?"

With astounding yeses, the group is back on the same page. Officer Rafter peeks his head in and shares the tip line for Paul is active, but so far, no one can verify his whereabouts. Some of his co-workers called the line asking about him. The police impounded Pauls' car from the courthouse lot. No one touched it since Paul parked. The plainclothes detective assigned to the vehicle stated no one even glanced inside the truck as they passed it.

Once Rafter finishes his updates, Larkin leads the group into their next step. He asks each member to call residents for an interview. The house manager will work with each of us to accommodate the interviews back to back. "There is no time to waste. We don't know the killer's intentions once this picture is complete."

The past interviews are in a stack at the end of the conference table. Each member takes two and starts from the beginning. Digger takes the first two known murders and asks Ellie, "You didn't see the scene on the first two murders, right?"

Ellie thinks back to the beginning of this mess and answers, "my first scene was with Beck, and if memory serves me, it was the fourth scene." All eyes in the room turned down at the mention of Beck. "I reviewed the files, but I didn't survey the scenes in person. Beck worked the first scene, but it remains a cold case. There were no witnesses and no DNA found."

"Is it strange why Chopper didn't mention the first victim living at his house? Or maybe it was a long time ago, and he didn't remember."

"Digger, I think I would remember a resident's murder. With Chopper having the house for decades, you hope all his residents mean something to him." Bob expounds.

"Me too, Bob. A halfway house can be a determining factor for a guy's life. Chopper and the rest of the house owners have a special place in their hearts for these young people that pass through their doors. We heard that as Chopper told us about Jose. So, why didn't he mention it? It seems odd to me unless Beck never followed up on the halfway house portion of the case."

Ellie's eyebrow lifts, "I thought Beck's file was thin. He worked the evidence, but he marked it as a cold case when it didn't pan out. The victim had no known relatives, so no one was hounding the police for a resolution to the crime."

Larkin remarks, "are you saying you don't feel he thoroughly worked the case?"

Taken aback by Larkin's tone, Ellie replies, "I'm not saying that all, but the file doesn't offer much in the way of information. There were no witness statements in the files."

"Its possible Beck had more going on than anyone knew because it looks like he had been battling his demons for a while. It's a shame he didn't talk to someone about it." Larkin's eyes were downcast and with a softer tone.

Digger brought the conversation back around to the past interviews. "The interviews we had which struck me as odd were the ones with Titus and Zachary. What about the other members? Do any of those have red flags on them? If so, we can start with those as our first interviews and then pick up the rest."

"Sounds like a plan, Digger. While we were talking, I pulled the files with red flags, and we have eleven. Titus is one of ours. He's the guy who doesn't speak much to anyone but Chopper. He stays in his room, which is on the second floor, and it faces the backyard. Titus runs errands for Chopper, and he works at a hardware store." Larkin read from the file notes. Then he flips to Zachary. "The only obvious fact about Zachary is hatred for law enforcement, and that makes me wonder. Both Titus and Zachary favor our description. With Zachary's feelings, we need to get him on the interview board now."

Larkin marks each file with a degree of urgency. These guys require a second interview. The questions will be more robust as the task force runs out of time to find a killer with a knack for carving people.

Chapter 18

Ellie's email notification sounds, and as she opens the email, she states in a high-pitched voice, "Digger, the email from genealogy about the male skull arrived."

He rolled his chair next to Ellie, eager to witness the results. The skull opened on the screen, and a name appeared below it, Harold Anderson of Marion County, West Virginia. Further down the page, there were additional notes. Harold married Loraine Anderson. No mention of a maiden name for Loraine and no children. "Can we find out if the Anderson's and the Teeter's are related?" Digger poses the question to Ellie.

"Let's try. I'll enter the query, and then we wait again."

After Ellie taps the enter button, they set about calling house managers for second interviews. Digger dials for Terry as Zachary stays with him. He suggests letting him contact Zachary for the discussion. Zachary is jumpy around law enforcement. It would be best coming from him. Digger obliges and requests a return call later in the day.

Ellie calls Chopper for Titus. Chopper mimicked Terry's request. Now, Ellie and Digger wait for return calls for the two most prominent suspects. While they wait, Ellie reviews the blood spatter from past crimes. She likes to keep the information fresh. Digger dives into Titus' interview. Nothing stands out. However, with his description and attitude, he has the potential of being their killer.

Digger asks Larkin if the task force has current photos of Zachary and Titus. Larkin shakes his head, "No, but why would you want those?"

"I thought dropping by the mechanic shop and showing off the pictures could help. If the shop owner can identify the visitor, we might have a primary suspect. Then, we have to prove it."

Eyebrows raised and a grin, Larkin plucks his phone from his pocket. "Rafter, I need you."

Rafter trots into the conference room. "What do you need, Larkin?"

"We need current photos of Zachary and Titus. Can we get them? Digger wants to stop in at the mechanic shop and see if the owner can identify either guy as the visitor he saw."

"I don't think photos are in their files, but I can handle it, and I'll stop over to the mechanic shop and speak with the owner." Rafter offers.

"Thanks, Rafter. Has the tip line produced any leads yet?"

"Nothing viable. Paul is a ghost." Rafter lowers his head and walks out of the room.

With no response from the house managers, Larkin suggests a trip to a hardware store. The same store where Titus works. The team stands as Larkin explains his idea. "I would like to see if this guy acts differently at work than in person. As a customer, I wouldn't like a service person helping me who didn't offer a smile."

"Ditto. I refuse to buy anything from a salesperson without a smile." Ellie states.

The ride to the hardware store took them into the quadrant where Paul went missing. Digger picks up on the coincidence first. "You all realize we're in the same vicinity where Paul went missing, right? I wouldn't mind taking a walk to the courthouse on the same route as Paul. Something might pop."

Ellie perks up, "I'll walk with you Digger after we stop in the store. This visit will give insight into the boy's personality and if he changes with the situation."

Larkin ends his call with Bob as they reach the lot. This store is active. There are only a few slots open. Larkin backs into a space, then they exit the vehicle.

Digger and Ellie walk through the garden center, pointing out flowers of their choice. "If I ever get a house, I want flowers in the front and a place for hanging baskets. Vibrant colors are my favorite for the front, so anyone driving by can enjoy them with me." Ellie's eyes have a far way look to them.

"Why, Ellie Masters, are you daydreaming?" Digger whispers in her ear, then he plants a soft kiss on her cheek.

He watches as the redness creeps up Ellie's neck. "I suppose I am, Digger. It's fun to dream. Everyone should dream a little."

"How about we work on that dream of yours? We could find a house in a quiet section of town somewhere and make it ours." Digger asks without losing eye contact. Sweat beads up along his upper lip as he waits for an answer.

"Are you serious, Digger? You want to buy a house together. That's a gigantic step for us. We'll sit and discuss it once we finish the case." Ellie states, but her insides melt. She wraps her arms around his neck and whispers, "I like that plan."

Ellie turns toward Larkin's voice and waits until he joins the pair. "Here you are. No one can find Titus. He's on the clock too, and his manager is mad. If you two want to walk toward the courthouse, I'll pick you up. I'll hang around here for thirty minutes as that should be ample time for your walk."

Digger takes Ellie's hand, and they walk to the courthouse. Digger glances from one side of the road to the other. The hardware store is more extensive than it looks. It's a city block deep with rows of outside products. This store sells gravel, mulch, stone, pine straw, and the list continues. Heavy machines run in the back of the store, loading enormous trucks for delivery. Digger wonders if Titus works in the back. It would be easy to hide in all the products.

The walk took twenty minutes with a couple of stops for Ellie to peer into the windows. The sidewalks need repair but are still usable, and some stores need a fresh coat of paint. But otherwise, the area seems acceptable. Now, wonder where Paul is? There is nowhere to hide between the courthouse and the hardware store.

Ten minutes after arriving at the courthouse, Larkin pulls to a stop. "Titus never showed. The manager checked with another worker and said Titus called for the day off today because Chopper is giving him a congratulatory dinner for his release."

"Can we stop by Choppers? We can act as if this is a surprise visit." Ellie suggests.

Larkin answers his phone and listens to Rafter to share his visit to the mechanic shop. The owner remembers Rafter from the scene, but he can't place Zachary or Titus at the shop. He thinks the visitor was larger, and he refers to Zachary and Titus as skinny.

"Unbelievable." Digger rests his head on the seat. Ellie turns around to face him and pats him on the knee.

Ellie shares their walk with Larkin. Digger adds his comments about the size of the hardware store and the activity in the back. Larkin admits he knows nothing about the back of the store. When he leaves, he turns in the opposite direction to search that side of the store. After the turn at the next light, stores dot the street. So, the store takes up a city block on one side, but other stores take space on the other side.

Larkin pulls away and heads in Chopper's direction. Nothing like a surprise visit at a farewell dinner. Chopper's house is quiet on the outside as the team pulls into the lot. We hear voices in the house's backyard. "Are we interrupting a cookout?" Digger asks.

"Maybe they will invite us to stay," Larkin replies with a half-grin and a chuckle.

Larkin knocks on the locked front door. No one comes forth, so he does it again with extra gusto. A different guy opens the door for us. "We're here to see Chopper and Titus. Are they around?" Larkin's tone belies authority.

Without explaining, the guy turns and heads off down the hallway. Larkin glances back and walks inside, followed by the team. Everyone is outside enjoying the weather. Chopper spots the team standing at the backdoor and walks to greet them. He invites the group to come out and join the festivities. "We are celebrating two releases this week. One cake for Titus and one for Damon. Although Damon hasn't made it yet."

Ellie watches Titus during the exchange, and he carries an odd expression. His eyes are cold and hard to read. He glances at Chopper once when he mentions Damon, and then his eyes lower. Titus doesn't offer a handshake or a nod to anyone.

"Can we speak with you and Titus for a moment, Chopper? It shouldn't take long, and then you can enjoy the rest of your night."

Once the group finds a chair at the kitchen table, Chopper is excited about Titus' release. He asks Titus about his new residence and if it is move-in ready. Titus nods in agreement. Chopper continues by saying Damon and Titus will live in the same apartment complex. Larkin and Digger ask a few follow-up questions but learn nothing of value. Titus will become a mentor at Chopper's while maintaining employment at the hardware store.

At the meeting conclusion, Ellie adds, "does anyone know Damon's whereabouts?"

Chopper answers, "he is late sometimes from work. He'll show."

With that, the group drives back to headquarters. Paul remains on the team's mind as no one has offered information on his whereabouts. Somewhere between the courthouse and the hardware store, Paul vanished. The possibility amazes Digger. With so many cameras and people in town, how could someone not notice Paul?

Digger and Ellie enter the conference room, not realizing Watson sits at the window. He turns around and faces the duo, "how did it go with Titus?"

Ellie shrieks when Watson speaks, then she states. "You scared me half to death. Why are you tucked in the corner?"

"I'm battling the media again. They're requesting a news conference, and I continue to push back. Since the Beck incident, we haven't had one, and I don't want to relive that fiasco. What are your thoughts?"

Digger steps forward, "It's whatever you think. However, you know the media. If you don't give them what they want, it might get worse than doing it now and getting it behind you."

Watson's head bobs as he considers Digger's words. "You might be right. I'll call Kelly and get her opinion."

Ellie looks at Digger, "Like she will say no."

Watson grins at Ellie, "that's my point."

Digger chuckles as he turns to see Rafter standing in the doorway. "Nothing new on Paul, Digger. We're still trying."

"I don't think you'll hear anything different, Rafter. Paul vanished somewhere between the hardware store and the courthouse. Ellie and I walked the route today, and we can't determine the exact area he went missing. There are stores on the route we took. Can we have a patrol officer stop in the stores and ask the workers if they recognize Paul? My guess is it will be a waste of time, but it's a try."

"I'll make it happen, Digger," Rafter answers his phone on the way out the door.

Larkin replaces Rafter in the room, "What's the update?"

"Nothing good. Rafter has nothing new. Watson discusses another news conference with Kelly."

Larkin stammers at the idea of another news conference. "I received a voice mail from Silas. Has anyone spoken to him today?"

Everyone shakes their head, and Digger shows concern for Silas's call. "Call him now. Let's see what he wants."

Larkin dials the phone, and Silas answers on the first half ring. Everyone's attention sharpens when they hear Silas's tone. "How's the investigation? Any new updates?"

Glances around the group, then Larkin updates Silas on the investigation, which takes seconds since nothing new has transpired. Larkin questions Silas on the real reason for the call.

Silas clears his throat, "I'm worried about Tara. She is a nervous wreck, and she refuses protection. The situation doesn't stress Oscar, but Tara talks about it constantly."

"We can't make her accept protection, Silas. You know that. When you leave for the day, can you travel in pairs?"

"Oscar and I do what we can, but with our case times set for us, we can't always be with her. Is there a plainclothes detective that could monitor her travels indiscreetly? I don't want her mad I pried into her life."

Larkin pauses, and Watson answers Silas. "Silas, this is FBI Special Agent Watson. We'll make it happen. I'll secure anonymous protection for Tara."

"Thanks. I appreciate it. Just don't tell her, I asked. Now, one more thing. Over the last two days, someone left notes on my car windshield that are a tad disturbing. I have them in my office if you want to see them. The notes state someone watches me. I don't know if they are supposed to scare me or what, but I thought you needed to be aware."

Digger jumps in, "Two days, Silas. You've gotten notes for two days, and you are just now mentioning it. Why would you take the chance?" Digger runs his fingers through his hair and rubs his temples.

Watson clarifies, "Let me make sure I understand this conversation. You called us asking for protection for Tara when you are the one getting threatening notes. Right?"

"Pretty much sums it up." Silas states.

"We're coming to the courthouse to collect the notes. Can you tell us where you park?" Larkin asks.

"Come on over. I'll wait in my office. There is always something to do."

The group climbs in the vehicle in awe. Few people are more concerned about someone else's safety than their own unless their family. Silas has a unique view of life, and Digger likes him more and more.

"Silas is one of a kind. He worries about Tara before he even tells us about the notes. That says a lot about the person." Digger points out.

Ellie and the group agree. "He acts as if Tara is his daughter. Is she? When he introduced her, he didn't mention it."

"It seems to me Silas is just looking out for her. Maybe he has a parental relationship with her." Digger throws out there.

Watson calls Larkin and requests details on the public defender's vehicles and location in the parking lot. The group listens as Larkin explains they are turning into the lot and will have the information shortly. "Watson works fast. Doesn't he?" Larkin asks on his way to the courthouse door.

Silas is true to his word. Files cover his desk as he waits on the team. "Come on in and take a seat. Let me dig out the notes. I put them in an envelope and stuffed them in the back of the drawer."

A few seconds later, Silas produces a brown envelope with a tie on the back. He unwinds the tie, and the notes slide onto his desk. He points to the notes in order. Both were on unlined white paper and black ink. Anyone could have written these.

"Did anyone touch the notes?" Larkin questions as he places the notes back into the envelope.

"No one other than me. I plucked the first one out before I realized what it was, and the second time, I used a tissue."

"That's good, Silas. We'll take this back to headquarters and let the crime lab tackle it. Can you tell us the year, make, model, and color of your car,

225

Tara's, and Oscar's? Watson is working on a protection detail for all three of you. We don't pick favorites, Silas."

"Understood. The public defenders park in the same general area, so the location shouldn't be an issue. I can show you on a map."

Silas plucks a paper map of the courthouse property layout from his desk drawer and circles the parking lot area they discussed in red marker. This area sits off to the side of the building, making it easy to target a vehicle without being seen. With the tall trees and shrubs encompassing the landscape around the lot, no one would notice a stranger walking the lot.

After studying the red circle on the map, Larkin suggests a different parking area. "Can you shift your parking to this lot? This one would give our guys an unobstructed view of your vehicles."

"I don't see why not. Tara and Oscar left for home already. I can share this info with them tonight. Our arrival time varies daily, depending on the caseload and meetings. It's between eight and ten every morning, Monday thru Friday."

"Is your home address listed anywhere someone could get it with a couple of clicks?" Digger asks.

"I own my home, so that information is in the tax assessor's office. The same for the other two. Why did you ask Digger? Do you think this killer would show up at one of our homes?"

"I'm unaware of how far this killer might go to complete his quest. The question helps us in fact-gathering. We might decide to have a plainclothes officer at your residence too. The decision remains open." Digger explains.

Ellie steps closer to Silas, "Would you review your cases, past and current, and determine if anyone strikes you as odd? They could be mad at the world, quiet and calculating, or verbally abusive."

Silas looks up at Ellie, "that will be a lengthy list. But I can get it for you if you think it will help."

"An extensive list, Silas?"

Chapter 19

"A long list, Ellie. These guys lived through a hard childhood before they got to me. Some have no family, and once released from the halfway house, they are on their own. They don't have an accountability partner to keep them on the straight and narrow road. A few are lucky enough to escape their past, but the others fall back into their old ways. However, their subsequent arrest sends them to prison without a stop at a halfway house."

"Interesting evaluation, Silas. I've never looked at the system like that before. Halfway houses give the offender a slight chance for rehabilitation. Chopper has a few guys eager for their release dates."

Silas clicks keys on his laptop, and a lengthy spreadsheet opens. "Here is my list of offenders. This is a years' worth of names. It would take hours to revisit each offender. Can you narrow the focus?" Silas turns the computer toward them for proof.

The team members glance at each other, and Larkin enlightens the group. "We have a guy's description seen at the mechanic shop and a similar one from the restaurant. Younger male, dirty blond hair, Caucasian, around six feet in height. The witnesses added this guy wore baggy clothes."

"Well, the clothes description won't help as many of the younger generations wears droopy clothes. Age will work, though. I can also search for hair color and race. Let's see how many return."

The group members hang around for a little while as Silas works on his list. He's not a computer genius, but he keeps plugging until he gets what he wants. "Here you go. The list comprises thirty-two folks that fit your description. I stopped at age twenty-five, which might be too old, but you can omit them." His printer churns out the pages for the team.

"Come on, Silas. We'll walk you to your car and follow you home. Thanks for your help." Larkin stretches his arm toward the door.

Everyone files through the door and notices the office is dark and quiet on the way to the lobby. Ellie gets a strange feeling as if someone watches their movement. Her eyes search every nook and cranny as they head to the elevator. Her neck hairs bristle at the thought of the cramped elevator car traveling down several floors. She's never feared an elevator before now. Why the change?

Ellie sees a shadow pass the doors as the elevator door closes, but the opening is too small to see the figure. In the door's reflection, Ellie makes eye contact with Digger. Just as Ellie's fear registers with him, the elevator slams to a halt, throwing everyone into the walls and onto the floor. Silas slams into the back wall, and Ellie crumples to the floor, landing on Larkin. Digger holds his left shoulder from the wall impact.

"Is anyone hurt?" Larkin asks as he rubs his knee.

"I should ask you, Larkin, since you broke my fall," Ellie states while trying to help Larkin stand.

Larkin tried to put his weight on his knee, but it buckled, and he almost met the floor again. "Great. Now is not the time for an injury. Wonder what caused the car to stop so suddenly? Digger, help me open the door. If we are close enough to a floor, we might shimmy out of here."

Silas and Ellie watch Larkin and Digger pull at the door opening. They work themselves into a sweat, and the doors refuse to budge. Digger presses the alarm button in the panel, and nothing happens. Ellie snatches the phone off the cradle, nothing. They share a look.

Larkin slides down the back wall into a sitting position. "Let me try a cell phone call." He studies the screen. "One bar of service. Pray, this call gets out." The others hold their breath as he makes a call to police headquarters. The answering service answers the ring on the non-emergency line. Larkin leaves a message. Digger texts Watson, but the text goes unread.

Ellie holds her phone in the air as she searches for a signal. "Hey, guys, it looks like the signal is stronger up there." She points to the ceiling. "This elevator doesn't have a hatch that I can see. Doesn't the county or city code require it?"

Larkin surveys the ceiling. "There's the latch. They camouflaged it into the ceiling tile. I can't reach it. Digger, can you try?"

As grunts and sighs escape from Digger's mouth, he succumbs to the trial. "I can't either. But, if we lift Ellie, she might reach it."

"Come over here, Ellie. Let's try it. Otherwise, I'm not sure what to do."

Larkin and Digger interlock their fingers together and lowers them for Ellie to step into. She grabs both men for stability as they raise her in the air. Ellie quickly reaches the latch, but she can't open it. She twists, turns, and slides the lock, but the door won't open. "Uh, guys, I smell smoke up here. It smells like burning rubber."

Silas yells out. "Try your cell phone while you are up there. Maybe the signal is better."

"Good idea, Silas. Do you have your phone, Ellie?"

"No, I put it back in my bag. Hand me yours, Digger. You have Watson on speed dial."

Digger pulls his phone from his pocket while holding Ellie in the air. He hands it up to her, and she snatches it while holding onto the wall.

"Yes!" Ellie screams. "There are two bars of service up here."

The first call is to Watson. He doesn't answer, so she leaves a message. Next, she tries Rafter. Same for him. "Why doesn't anyone answer their phones? I'm calling 911."

Ellie coughs when the smoke enters through the ceiling. After she ends the call, the men lower her to the floor. Her face is red and blotchy, with sweat running down the sides. Digger finds a napkin in her bag and wipes her face with it.

The foursome leans back against the elevator walls and wait. Finally, the air becomes so sparse that talking is painful, so they stop. They shut their eyes and concentrated on surviving this ordeal. Would someone sabotage the elevator, and how would they know which one they would ride?

Ellie passes out first. The guys hang on with shallow breaths. Smoke pours into the car from the ceiling and swirls on its way to the floor. With each breath, they inhale more smoke, and with that, life ebbs away. Digger's last recollection is sitting next to Ellie with her head resting on his shoulder.

Digger stirs when he hears loud noises and yelling. He doesn't remember his location until he shakes his head and looks around. He sees Larkin and Silas out cold. Ellie is also out. Digger determines the noise is coming from above the car, but something slams into the car from the side.

A man's deep voice penetrates the car, "this is the city fire department. We're working to free you from the car. Is everyone okay in there?"

With the thick smoke, Digger's throat closes as he opens his mouth to speak. He coughs a few times, then squeaks, "we're alive. I have three unconscious adults with me. Hurry." Digger lays his head back and succumbs to the smoke again.

The fire department works to free the group from the elevator. With the group trapped between floors, it makes extraction difficult. Firefighters try to gain entry from above, but a snapped cable blocks the roof hatch. These cables are heavy, and it takes multiple people to move them. Lieutenant Primton instructs his crew to rig a pulley system to lift the line from the car. After a lengthy delay, the first fire department crew member opens the ceiling hatch into the car.

"Lieutenant Primton, we have four adults, three men, and one woman. All appear unconscious from here. Send in four baskets. I don't see any of them walking out. Call for extra ambulances."

Forty-five minutes later, the firefighters lift all four persons from the car. The EMS workers placed oxygen on each individual and opened it to 100%. Slowly, Digger opens his eyes and glances around. He couldn't sit up, but he answered questions for the lieutenant.

Watson, Bob, and Rafter run over to Digger's gurney when they notice him speaking with the lieutenant. "Digger, we're here. We'll follow the ambulances."

Digger didn't respond except to lift his thumb. His head turns just enough to see Ellie being loaded into an ambulance. Then, his eyes close.

Watson places his hand on Lieutenant Primton's arm as he introduces himself. "Can you tell me what happened here? Your four patients are in the middle of a serial murder case. Were they targeted?"

"It looks like the cable holding the car snapped. We'll take another look at it to make the final determination. Your friends are lucky. The lady appears to be in worse shape. The smaller you are, the harder smoke is on a body. However, I foresee everyone making a full recovery. Let me have your contact information, and I'll send you the final report."

"I appreciate it, Lieutenant Primton. Thanks for your work here today." Watson shakes hands with the lieutenant then hands him a business card. And steps away.

Rafter ponders the events. "Primton, can you check the cables on the other cars while you inspect the damaged one?"

The lieutenant nods in agreement and wanders off to meet his crew. Rafter fears the perpetrator damaged all the elevator cables, and more accidents will occur. So it's better to inspect now and prevent others.

With Ellie, Digger, Larkin, and Silas in the hospital, Watson paces the emergency room waiting for word on their conditions. Bob sits in the room's corner, making calls and answering emails. Watson's boss expects an update from him, as does Kelly. But, instead, the elevator malfunction unnerves everyone.

Watson looks at Bob, "where's Rafter? I thought he was following the ambulances."

"He stayed back to speak with Lieutenant Primton after the last inspections. For unknown reasons, the other three elevator car cables concern him. I'm unaware if he knows something or if he's just suspicious. Don't forget to call your boss. He's attempted to call you several times." Bob lowers his head to read an email and then says as an afterthought, "Kelly is trying to reach you too."

A grin spreads across Watson's face as his thoughts turn to Kelly. Where is she? I know she heard about the accident at the courthouse. There were news vans in the lot when the ambulances left for the hospital. Wonder why she said nothing to him at the scene?

The ER doctor burst into the waiting room, asking for Watson. Both Watson and Bob face the doctor expecting an update. "All four friends are doing fine. But, as a precaution, I would suggest they stay overnight for observation. Ellie presents wheezing when talking without oxygen. If we can keep her overnight, the extra hours on oxygen will do her body wonders. Silas is coming around but slower than the rest."

"Thank you, doctor. They had us scared. When can we see them?" Watson asks.

"Chet is asking for you now. If you come with me, I'll show you the way."

Watson and Bob grab their gear and follow the doctor down a winding corridor. Finally, he admits them through the back door into a quadrant of beds. He points out the occupants of each room. Watson begins in Digger's. Digger appears asleep as Watson and Bob slip in.

"Where have you been, Watson? We called you from the elevator. Is everyone okay?"

Watson raises his hand, "I got your message, but by the time I called 911, someone beat me to it. Everyone is okay. Ellie gasps from the smoke inhalation, Larkin is fine, and Silas is a little slower recovering, but he'll be fine too. The ER doctor is admitting you all overnight for observation."

"I need not stay here. I feel lightheaded, but other than that, I'm good." Digger replies.

"You're staying. Don't argue." Bob states with his hands on his hips.

Digger lays back on his pillows. "Then where's supper? I'm hungry."

A nurse pokes her head from behind the curtain, "we're working on it. The meal trays are on the way upstairs."

"There you go, Digger. I guess you heard that. Now, did any of you see anyone in the courthouse while you were there?" Watson questions.

"Not a soul. After we finished with Silas, we told him we would follow him home for safety's sake. As we left his office, the rest were dark. We were the last ones to leave. I remember standing at the elevators waiting for one to arrive when I noticed Ellie's expression. I couldn't tell if something scared her or what troubled her. We walked into the elevator and turned to face the door when Ellie gasped and pointed at the door. When the doors shut, she turned to me and said, she thinks someone was out there. Then the jolt slammed us to the ground when the elevator halted."

"Did Ellie identify the person before the doors closed?"

"Nope. She said she saw someone, but she didn't have time to tell me who it was before the crash. Then we tried to open the ceiling hatch. At least Ellie called 911 before we passed out. Any word from Lieutenant Primton on the cables? I'd like to know if it was sabotage or a freak accident."

Bob glances at his phone, "no word yet. They were entering the building to begin the inspection as we were leaving. He stated he would call Watson this evening."

Watson shares with Digger he's stepping into Ellie's room next, then Larkin, followed by Silas. With Silas struggling to wake up, he wants to save his visit until the last. Ellie sleeps as the men walk into the room. Groggy, she reaches for Watson's hand. They chat for a minute, but her wheezing prevents her from saying too much. Watson explains the situation and leaves her room for Larkin. Watson and Bob interrupt his snack as they enter.

"Well, I guess the food means you'll make it."

"Yes, I will. Except for a slight cough and headache, I'm fine. You don't have a steak dinner tucked into your bag?" Larkin asks with a smile.

"I didn't have time to stop for a meal when I listened to Ellie's plea for help because I assumed the worse, and it was the longest drive ever. We're glad you all made it out alive. It sounds like a hairy incident."

"I've experienced nothing like it. First, the elevator slammed to a stop. The alarm and the phone didn't work, and the cell service was weak. Digger and I lifted Ellie to the ceiling to see if she could open the hatch. That didn't work, which in hindsight, was a good thing. The smoke entering would have been one-hundred times worse. She found a spot towards the ceiling that allowed for great cell service for an emergency call."

Bob shakes his head in disbelief as Larkin describes the scene. Watson's phone rings as he plucks it from his pants pocket. "It's Lieutenant Primton from the fire department," Watson answers the call then steps away from the bed. Bob and Larkin listen to the conversation even though it's one-sided. The guys watch as Watson grips the phone until his knuckles turn white.

Watson turns with a red face and neck veins protruding. "The elevator crash was deliberate. Both elevators on the crash side had cut cables. Someone stopped the elevators on the opposite side by hand in between floors, so they were inoperable. Both elevators would have produced the same outcome."

"Now, the killer is coming for us," Larkin whispers.

Chapter 20

The men stand in Larkin's room and consider the case from a different angle. Has the killer completed his picture? If so, where are the bodies? No one has reported a recent murder. So if his murder spree is over, what's next?

"I want the surveillance video feed from the courthouse- now." Barks Larkin. "The guy was in the courthouse. He must be on camera."

With his phone to his ear, Watson calls the courthouse security team and requests the video feed emailed to Bob. He emphasized urgently. Watson and Larkin discuss a plan for when the hospital releases the foursome. Larkin expresses concern for the safety of the public defenders and how they planned to have a plainclothes detective guard the three public defenders. Now, the plan might change if everyone stays at a safe house. Although Silas will refuse protection, maybe the others will not.

Officer Rafter works overtime, assigning guards to Tara and Oscar. Oscar is at home with his family, so we posted his guard outside. Oscar lives in a neighborhood with houses on all four sides. So it would be difficult for an intruder to make their way inside unseen. But Tara lives in a downtown condo, and she hasn't answered her phone yet.

Watson answers Rafter's call, and he listens as Rafter explains the guard's situation. A bad feeling washes over Watson as he listens to the bit about Tara. When Rafter takes a breath, Watson asks,

"Does Tara have a significant other? Friends, family in the area? We need to locate her now."

"I can't answer, Watson. I'm not familiar with Tara. Can you peek in on Silas and ask him? If you prefer not to, then I understand."

Watson follows Rafter's advice and walks across the room to where Silas rests. "Silas, how are you feeling?"

"Good. Do we know what happened to the elevator yet? My gut tells me it wasn't a freak accident. Elevators don't just drop at a whim."

A pause before he answers, "You're right, Silas. The accident was deliberate. But now, we are looking for Tara. Do you know where she is? We've checked her house, and she isn't answering her phone."

Silas shakes his head in annoyance. "Our plan tonight was for me to call Oscar and Tara to discuss protection and get their vehicle information, but now we'll have to go through the DMV. If something happens to Tara, I'm unsure what I'll do. She is like a daughter to me. Find her, Watson."

A text alert sounds from Watson's phone. He shares with Silas, "Rafter has a BOLO out for Tara's vehicle. Do you have any of her friends or family contact information?"

"Her family is out of state. I never asked about gathering contact information. I'm her emergency contact with the county. Check the gym. Sometimes she stops there on her way home. I don't know the name, but it's on the next block over from her condo."

Fingers fly across the keyboard as Watson sends a text to Rafter explaining the gym. Rafter's reply was swift. A patrol car is en route.

Agitation brought on a coughing fit, and the nurses shooed Watson out of Silas' room. Of course, it's Watson's fault Silas coughed like that, but he must find Tara, and Silas is closer to her than anyone else.

Bob shrugs his shoulders as Watson hurries out of the nurse's way. "Watson, we have the courthouse video. Do you want Larkin to watch it with us? We can view it on my laptop."

Watson waves at Bob for him to follow. As the two men enter Larkin's curtained room, he sits up straighter in the bed. The men's faces gave it away. Something is happening, and it's troublesome. "What's wrong? I can tell by your faces. Don't hide it just because I'm lying in a bed. Get me out of here."

"We can't do that. We need the doctor's release, and he refuses to sign until tomorrow. So you're stuck until then, but we have two things. First, we haven't located Tara. The police are out in full force, searching for her vehicle. Second, we have the video from the courthouse. Do you feel up to watching it with us?"

"Start the video. Let's identify our culprit."

241

The video starts in slow motion. Every person walking through the front door is on camera. They pass through metal detectors, and they empty their pockets into bins. With the security precautions at the door, how did this person gain access to the elevator banks?

With a pointed finger, Larkin says, "stop the video. He looks familiar, but I can't say from where. We need to ask the group and see if they can remember the face. Notate the time stamp and then continue."

The video is lengthy since it encompasses the entire workday. No one else stood out as a potential suspect. How can someone gain access to the elevators without tools? There is no way a set of tools will pass the security team.

With a head nod, "Are there cameras for the maintenance entrances? The guy could have slipped in with a work crew." Bob picks up his phone and fires off a text to the security chief. "We'll know shortly about the cameras."

Larkin laid his head back on his pillow. His face is pale, and his breathing is shallow. "Get a nurse, Bob. Something is going on with Larkin."

Holding his laptop and phone, Bob trots to the nurse's station as he asks for help. A cute petite nurse leads Bob back to Larkin's room. "We're transferring your friends upstairs for the night. Mr. Larkin, can you hear me?" The nurse balls her fist and places it in the middle of his chest and presses while she rubs. Larkin grunts but doesn't speak. Next, the nurse turns the oxygen back to 100%.

Finally, after a few minutes, Larkin opens his eyes and looks around.

"What happened? The last thing I remember was the video." Larkin exclaims as he stares at Watson.

The nurse stated his oxygen level dropped so low he passed out. She explains again they'll move the foursome to an upstairs floor for the night. Smoke inhalation takes a severe toll on the lungs, and it takes time for the body to restore the needed oxygen levels. The third-floor nursing supervisor prepares the group's arrival since Watson requests they be in the same area because he doesn't want anyone to be without police protection.

Watson and Bob moved to the area away from the rooms. They want the group to rest while they digest the newest information. Scribbling notes on his pad, Watson writes the next steps. First is Tara's location. Next, the person in the video needs identifying, and then the video from the maintenance entrance. Watson appreciates the activities so far, but he expects to capture the killer soon with their recent information.

Just as Watson thought all was well, Bob leans over as he reminds him about the news conference. A huge sigh escapes Watson's lips. "Really, Bob? Things are in motion to capture this killer, and you remind me of a news conference."

"It's set for tomorrow morning at nine. I suggest moving it to the afternoon or waiting until the day after. We need the team healthy even though Ellie need not take part in it. We can ask Kelly to help with the video again. If this killer caused the elevators to fall, he would attend this conference. We haven't released news of the accident victims yet. The public is aware of the elevator incident, but not the passengers, at least for now."

"Let's table the news conference for a day or two unless we need the public's help to locate Tara. Have you heard anything from Rafter yet? What about the security team for the other camera views?"

Bob checks his phone before replying, "nothing on Tara, and the security chief is gathering the video feed for us, and he'll send it to my email. My bet is the guy slipped in through the back door. I hope the camera caught him unaware, and we have a face. This guy is getting more and more aggressive."

Watson paces the small area, and it looks as if he is turning circles. Finally, after a few laps, he rubs his head and sits down. "Dizzy, Watson?" Bob asks and snickers.

"Funny, Bob. I'm walking outside to call Kelly. It would be nice if she made it to the courthouse and recorded the events for us." Watson stands, stretches, and walks through the back door of the emergency room. He turns his face to the sky and offers a prayer for Tara. She is too young to be murdered by some sadistic guy out for revenge.

Kelly answers on the first ring, "Watson, how are things with your team? I've wanted to call, but I didn't want to interfere."

"Things are good here. Everyone is recovering, and the doctors should release them tomorrow. The only issue right now is finding this killer. Were you at the courthouse? I didn't see you there, but I was busy. We were hoping you were there, and your cameraman recorded the visitors to the courthouse."

"We were at the courthouse. I'm not sure how much footage he got, but he recorded for a while. It took the fire department a while to work a plan for extraction. I had an interview with Lieutenant Primton once the ambulances left the scene, and he confirmed the elevator incident was not an accident."

"He did? Lieutenant Primton agreed to give me a little time before he confirmed it. Wonder what changed his mind? I'm preparing a press release for both the murders and the elevator incident. Would you be willing to cover it again and have your cameraman record for us again?"

Kelly pauses before she answers, "I changed Lieutenant Primton's mind. It only took a little persuasion to get him to confirm the incident. Yes, I would love to be at your press conference. Text me the time, place, and date, and we'll be there. When can we enjoy dinner together?"

Watson stammers as his concern lies with the killer, not dinner, although Kelly makes it challenging to say no. "There's that persuasion again, huh? I'll text you, Kelly. Thanks for your help."

As Watson enters the hospital, he faces his team in the hallway. "What's going on, Bob? I leave for five minutes, come back, and everyone in the hallway."

"They're moving the group to their rooms for the night. When they settle upstairs, we'll leave for dinner. A plainclothes detective arrives in fifteen minutes. He'll guard their rooms for the night."

Watson looks at his team and feels thankful no one succumbed to the smoke inhalation. Silas looks pale, but the others appear to be okay. Without information on Tara, Watson doesn't know which way to turn. Paul is still missing too. He tells himself to follow up with Rafter on the tip line. How can a person disappear from a city sidewalk?

An email alert sounds as Bob and Watson check their phones. Bob states, "I have the video from the maintenance entrance. Let's wait until the crew gets upstairs. Then we can watch it without interruption."

With everyone resting comfortably and protected, Bob opens his email for the video. The men sit in the hospital's corner waiting room, watching the video unfold. This video is the slowest of all. So few people use this door. Once the maintenance workers enter for their shift, the door stays shut. Then, three-quarters of the way through, a shadow crosses the camera. Both men straighten in their seats and get a little closer to the screen.

The video continues for a few minutes until the door opens, and a group of workers leaves for the day. They say their goodbyes to their co-workers, and as the last person leaves the screen, the door bumps, and a person walks inside. Bob stops the video in several places, but the person's face who enters later is unknown. Pieces of dirty blond hair poke out from his ball cap.

"Did you see the guy's hair? It's the same color as our description from the mechanic." Watson asks Bob.

"I see it. I think the description is spot on. Unfortunately, we've had too many sightings with this description. Should we change course again and shift to just the dirty blond hair?"

Watson considers the question before he answers. "Our concentration will be the guy with the dirty blond hair. He's our killer. I'm confident. Kelly's cameraman is sending over the video from the courthouse incident. I bet the killer was in the crowd wanting to see if any of the team died in the elevator."

The men pack their gear and stop by the crew's room once more before leaving for the day. Their guard is on duty, so there is nothing for Watson or Bob to do at the hospital. Watson has enough work waiting on him at headquarters with the press release, the tip line, and Tara. His gut clenches every time he thinks of her. Where could she be? Watson plans on greeting Tara in the morning at the courthouse unless he hears from her tonight.

Headquarters is active upon their arrival. Officer Rafter waves a message at Watson on his way into the room. Rafter joins the men in the room and explains his urgency. "The tip line received a call about Paul. The caller couldn't ID the person because he was wearing a hoodie. Paul did not appear to be in distress as he waited for his friend to make a purchase. After that, no sightings."

It fascinated Watson that after the store, Paul vanishes. Where is this store, and what's around it? Maybe the killer is holding Paul hostage in a warehouse or something. "Will someone find this store? I want to see the surroundings."

With satellite surveillance imagery, Rafter pulls the store location and shows the screen to Watson and Bob. "Isn't that the hardware store where Titus works?"

"I think so, but Larkin visited the store. I wasn't with them on that interview. So we need to confirm with Larkin before we do anything else." Watson clarifies.

"Rafter, is there any word on Tara? I'm getting worried. It's been hours since Silas left her a message. She should have retrieved it by now."

"The patrol officers stationed outside her place checked in a few minutes ago. Unfortunately, they haven't seen her, and her place remains dark." Rafter advises.

"If anything happens to Tara tonight, I want to hear it. The time doesn't matter. Bob and I will be here for an hour working on the press release."

Rafter leaves, and Watson paces while his mind never stills. Just as the men begin on the press release, Watson's email sounds. He glances at Bob and clicks it open. Kelly's cameraman sent the video. Deferring to the video, the men sit back and watch as the courthouse incident happens in real-time. The first pass-through was uneventful. On the second view, the men notice watchers matching the infamous description. Two young guys stand in the back of the crowd as the cameraman pans the front of the building. Since the cameraman stood toward the rear of the group, the video only shows the guy's back and the partial side of one guy.

"Another visual of a dirty blond guy. This is too much of a coincidence. The team will begin working with the description again. Starting with the folks we've already interviewed. Someone is not telling us something."

Bob mentions the press conference. He doesn't want to write it alone since this is the first one since Beck's suicide. They've uncovered a ton of information, but should they share it with the public? Tara and Paul are missing. The public hasn't heard about Tara yet, but they can share Paul's picture again. The courthouse incident is public now and confirmed by Lieutenant Primton that it was no accident.

Watson rubs his face and leans back in the chair, then sighs. Worry lines crease his forehead as he decides what to say in the press release. "Bob. Let's make this about the courthouse incident. Kelly will be at the news conference. She can add a snippet of Lieutenant Primton, confirming it was no accident in her report. We want the killer to know we have his description, and he should be in custody soon."

With his mouth hanging open, Bob stares at Watson. Then he clears his throat before he offers, "You're goading this guy. You'll put your team in the crosshairs. I'm not sure I agree with this tactic."

Both men sat in silence as they tried to agree on a press release. One is for prompting the killer, and the other is to play it soft. Acknowledge the courthouse incident but say the fire department pulled the individuals to safety. A few times, Bob disagrees with Watson, but he is not afraid to stand up either. Watson can sometimes jump without thinking about what he might hit.

"Write the release however you want. I'll agree with it. Drive me to the hotel, Bob. I'm tired. It's been a long day." Finally, Watson gives in to Bob's idea of the release, and he grins as he gathers his things.

Chapter 21

The following morning Ellie and Digger welcome a day without hospitals. They meet Larkin and Silas in the hallway. The group enters the elevator while surveying the interior, then presses the down button. Elevators will never be the same after their experience.

Bob picks them up outside the main entrance, and he drives to the hotel for Ellie and Digger. Larkin and Silas return to the courthouse for their vehicles. Silas insists on working, so he proceeds upstairs to his office. Larkin and Bob call for Watson since Tara is on their mind. Watson advises he is upstairs in the courthouse speaking with Tara. She visited a college friend and didn't know anyone searched for her until she returned to work this morning since she left her cell phone on her desk.

It relieved both guys to hear Tara is okay. Now, the only missing person is Paul. His disappearance is a complete mystery. The last time anyone saw him alive was at the store down the street from the hardware store. Larkin brings up a point, "Bob, could Paul be in the back lot of the hardware store? There is a lot of space and places people don't regularly visit."

"No one has suggested the store before. But, with the store so close, it becomes a distinct possibility." Bob replied.

Larkin nodded, then stated, "We're meeting with everyone this afternoon, and the hardware store will be a topic."

Bob receives a text, and he glances at it. "Watson approves the press release, so they set it for two this afternoon pending no intrusions. So this one will be short."

Larkin slides into his vehicle and heads to headquarters while Bob joins Watson at the courthouse.

When Larkin enters the conference room, Ellie and Digger study a laptop. He waits before he clears his throat. "Larkin. Look what we have. We finally have the missing bones identified and the relationships acknowledged. Harold and Loraine Anderson are related to the Teeter's. Loraine is Mrs. Teeter's mother."

"That's interesting. Someone murdered the owner of the home and the wife's parents and dumped them in the crawl space of the family home. Whoever killed these people is mean! Could it have been a child of the Teeter's or possibly a sibling of the Anderson's?" Larkin inquires.

"Our search produced no children born to the Teeter's. But that doesn't mean there isn't one floating around that is unaccounted for. The child might have changed their name for religious reasons or something." Digger states. The more he thinks about the child angle, the more he likes it.

"Ellie, can you search for siblings of Loraine Anderson?" Ellie clicks away at the laptop as she answers with a head nod.

Larkin sits at the table and jots notes in his pad. "Watson has a news conference set for two this afternoon. Your presence isn't required. So, you can remain here or go to the hotel."

Ellie peeks at Digger, not sure how to respond. Finally, she looks down and rubs her hands together before answering, "I'll stay here, but Digger is free to attend if he wants."

"We'll see how the day plays out, and then I can decide. My gut tells me to stay here with you." Digger says, then looks at Larkin as his head shakes.

Digger pulls out a notebook with scribbles in it. "My suggestion to re-interview Calon, Zachary, and Titus. Those three match our description, and Zachary and Titus were the odd acting guys. Calon seems personable, but I don't want to throw the others off by not including Calon since their friends. Calon lives in the smaller halfway house downtown if I remember correctly."

Everyone agrees with Digger's assessment that the halfway house is the connection. They must weed through many people to find the right one. Once they set their sights on a specific individual, they must have evidence to support their view. Without DNA from the scenes, this will be difficult, but not impossible.

While Watson gives the press release, Digger sets about making phone calls to the halfway houses for the three suspects. Chopper's home tops the list. After discussing with Chopper, he relents and shares Titus moved out yesterday to begin his new life. So, he recited Titus's cell phone number. Zachary is at work, and he takes a message for him because he refuses to give up Zachary's number since he's still a resident.

Next, Digger places a call to Calon's house. Hank, the house manager, expresses concern for Calon. No one has seen Calon for a couple of days now. Hank is meeting with a detective from his precinct to report a missing person. The police refused to take one yesterday since Calon is an adult. However, they have time requirements, and those are met at three this afternoon. Digger asks Hank for Calon's vehicle information as he wants to place a BOLO on the vehicle.

When the call ends, Digger rubs the back of his neck then looks up. All eyes are on him. "Calon is missing. Hank will make a missing person report this afternoon at three. I have Calon's vehicle information. Can Rafter issue a BOLO for it? I've got a bad feeling."

Ellie reaches for Digger's hand. "We can't lose another one, Digger. As soon as the conference is over, I'm sure Rafter will do it for us."

"Did I hear my name? I hope it was in a good context." Rafter says, grinning as he enters the room.

"We might have another murder. Calon, from Hank's house, is missing. I have his vehicle information. Can you issue a BOLO for it?" Digger's tone expresses his concern as worry lines increase on his forehead. "I realize you might not have time now, but after the news conference."

Rafter takes the paper and walks out of the room. Ten minutes later, he appears and advises the BOLO is out to all city-wide patrol cars. "What else can I do to help? Since the tip line isn't much help, I'm left empty-handed. No way I was going to the news conference without the BOLO. There have been too many deaths."

"We're waiting for Watson to finish the press conference. Kelly's cameraman is sending over the footage of the participants for us to view. We are hoping to spot someone we recognize."

"The news conference has ended. Bob was in the break room, pouring coffee last I saw him. I'm unsure of Watson's whereabouts, though." Rafter's belt radio crackles, waiting for a reply. When Rafter squeezes the radio and answers, a calm voice comes over the air and advises the vehicle from the BOLO has been located. The crime scene unit is en route.

Rafter spins his head to make eye contact with Digger. "You were right to be concerned, Digger." Then, he pushes the buttons on the radio, "Text me the address."

Once he receives the text, Rafter forwards it to Digger. "Want to come along, Rafter? You earned it. You can drive us." Ellie and Digger grab their gear and walk to the hallway. Their expressions show sadness but determination. Another murder, and for what?

The trio stands at the elevators when the door opens. They meet Watson. They share the news, and Watson's face turns red. "I'm coming too. I'll text Bob my location. He needs downtime anyway after he wrote the press release overnight."

Watson calls Larkin and advises him of the latest situation. Larkin stayed back at the conference to wait on the video footage. After Watson explains, Larkin is quiet. He is unsure of his words. How can this killer keep going? "Watson, send me the address. I'll meet you there."

This scene differs from the rest. Calon's car sat parked in the back lot of a bowling alley. A patrol officer spotted it yesterday while on patrol and assumed the owner worked in the bowling alley, so he didn't get out for a walk around.

The driver parked the car as if he's inside bowling. With the windows tinted, it makes it difficult to see inside. Calon experienced death inside the vehicle, but the door must have been open when someone fired the shots. The driver's window remains intact. Ellie inspects the inside of the vehicle and confirms the fact. The door was partially open when the killer fired at Calon. The bullet gauged out a portion of the seat upholstery at such an angle that it traveled to the rear passenger door.

Ellie points this out, and the crew disassembles the rear passenger door. A mangled bullet sits inside the door. The group's first piece of evidence. The investigators realize the find and spirit's lift.

Larkin takes a pen and lifts Calon's shirt to find a vertical line carved into the left side of his chest. With his face red, he turns and looks at the crew. There is no doubt their killer is still active. Ellie leans into Larkin, "we still have one piece of the picture missing." With that, Larkin steps away from the vehicle and looks around.

"I'm going to Hank's. He needs to know we have Calon."

"Larkin, I'll go with you. Rafter can drive the others to headquarters." Watson adds.

There is nothing more to see at the scene. But, Ellie and Digger want to revisit the picture because there is one piece still missing. So, where is it? Why hasn't someone found this body? "Somebody should have found the last piece of this puzzle weeks ago, right?" Digger questions Ellie.

"Yes. It should be another vertical line, but this one will be on the right side of the chest. A mirror image of Calon's." With eyebrows bunched, Ellie glances at Digger.

"Where is the other vertical line?" Digger questions as he takes hold of Ellie's hand. They walk to Rafter's vehicle and wait until he finishes his inquiry.

Rafter shares with the duo, the crime scene tech found tire tracks next to Calon's vehicle. They surmise this location was a meet. Calon knew his killer and felt safe enough to park behind a bowling alley. The tech thinks the tires are from a pickup truck. He'll need to get the cast back to the lab before he knows more.

Digger reads a text then alerts the team to the next item. "Watson wants us to return to headquarters and start on the video footage. Kelly is waiting for us."

At headquarters, Kelly waits in the lobby for us. We invite her inside the conference room, but she stalls when she finds out that Watson is not here. Digger offers to have Watson call her upon his return. The trio didn't share about Calon's death. That tidbit of information is for Watson or Larkin to divulge.

Rafter cues the video on the big screen, and we sit back to watch yet another news conference. There are a lot more people at this one, and they are becoming more vocal. Mostly women worried about their sons and the fear of not being able to protect them. Digger watches the conference intently when he sees a face. "Stop the video."

The outburst scared Rafter, and he missed the timing. "Back it up, Rafter, ten seconds."

After Rafter figures out the program and learns the backup mode, he recovers the face. "Who does that look like, Ellie? We've seen him somewhere."

"Um, I'm not sure. Is there a better picture of him? He looks like all the other young kids." Ellie states.

The face troubles Digger. He thumbs through a few of the files on the table. "Here. This is it. Titus Jett.

I knew he looked familiar. So, why is it at the news conference?"

"Because his friends are dying one by one, and he wants to know what the police are doing to catch the killer. Or he is the killer." Ellie says in a soft voice. "Do you think it's him?"

"I don't know, but I want to speak to him again, and Larkin needs to rattle his cage. Chopper gave me Titus's cell number, but he hasn't returned my call yet. Maybe he's at work. I might need a tool or two from his hardware store." Digger lifts his right eyebrow and glances at Rafter and Ellie.

Rafter reminds us Chopper indicated Titus doesn't have many friends. He's the one that stays to himself when he's at the house. "What are the chances of these guys meeting with Titus in their homes? Isn't that unlikely?"

"It depends on what he offers the guys or the premise for the meeting. They all had jobs, so that's not it." Digger paces as he thinks. He rubs the back of the neck and looks out the window. "Nothing comes to mind right now. Let's finish the video."

The rest of the video plays for the trio, and nothing pops. This was a brief conference compared to the others. One person asks about suicide, but Watson refuses to entertain it. A few of the TV reporters asked bland questions, and Watson handled those with ease.

Digger dials the number for Titus. Again, he leaves a voice mail. Next, he calls the hardware store.

Titus works tomorrow and would love to help a customer with a new tool purchase. Digger turns and faces his two co-workers. "I'm getting used to investigative work." He says with a huge grin.

"Well, Digger, I didn't know you had in you. Great thinking. So, tomorrow we visit Titus. What about Zachary? He was the other odd fellow."

Rafter calls for Zachary, and his call is easy as Zachary agrees to meet the team tomorrow after his shift around three. Digger and Rafter high-five feelings like they accomplished something. Digger's phone rings. When he glances at the number, his insides twist.

"Hi, Silas. Slow down. Start from the beginning." Digger listens as Silas describes his office. Rafter and Ellie watch Digger's face for any sign of distress. "Silas, Officer Rafter is with me. Hold on and let me ask."

Digger explains the situation. "Silas attended the press conference at headquarters. When he returned to his office, it was in shambles. Furniture tossed, picture frames broken, and notes taped to the wall. Can you take us over there and take a report for him? The man sounds bad."

Rafter nods and says, "absolutely, I'll take the report. Let's leave now. Tell him we will be there in fifteen minutes."

After Digger confirms Rafter is coming, Silas calms. While Digger finishes up with Silas, Rafter calls Watson and informs him of the new situation.

Watson and Larkin are driving back from Hank's halfway house. They'll go to the courthouse and meet Silas.

Everyone converges on Silas. He looks distraught. His face is red and sweaty, and he breathes rapidly. Ellie suggests EMS look at Silas before they let him go home. Silas refuses. He continues putting his office back in order. Rafter completes the report, but Silas doesn't want crime scene guys in his office because they'll spread fingerprint dust everywhere. He can't appear in court with files covered in dust.

The group helps arrange Silas's office. After a few minutes, Silas appears to calm down, but then he shows the note. He plops down into his leather desk chair and swivels it around, and points. In bold letters, a message states, "you are next. You cannot escape the Scales of Justice."

"What does that mean? Does anyone know?" Silas asks in a quivering voice.

Watson looks around at the group before he begins. He explains the meaning behind the Scales of Justice. No one has shared with Silas about the carvings. Silas only knew of the deaths. So, with the note, is Silas supposed to be the last victim of the picture?

"Let me get this straight. Whoever kills these guys carves pictures into their chest, and all the carvings together create a picture of the Scales of Justice. Incredible. Now, why would someone go to all the trouble?"

The group glances around the office. Ellie steps forward and explains the profile of the individual doing these things. She shares their thoughts that the guy feels wronged by the justice system and sets out for revenge.

"I've had many people in my day tell me how upset they are over their court outcome or which halfway house assignment. But murder? That's too much." Silas states as he shakes his head, trying to understand the killer's thought process.

Silas's statement triggers a question from Digger. "How often do guys get upset with you over a halfway house assignment?"

"Rarely. Most of those that get mad want to join a friend or something. Once they realize they can visit other houses, they tend to calm." Silas explains. "Well, thanks for coming. I'm tired, and I'm going home."

Larkin raises his hand. "You're not going home alone. Your choices are to stay with me until this over or have a detective stay with you at home."

Silas ponders the outcome. "No offense Larkin but I don't want to interrupt your home life, so send me a detective."

Everyone leaves together. Rafter drives Digger and Ellie back to headquarters while Larkin and Watson follow Silas home as a precaution. The notes stir fear in the group knowing the killer let himself into Silas' office. The killer is getting too close for comfort.

Larkin and Watson discuss the case while monitoring Silas. A traffic light separates the cars, and Silas never slows. Watson tries to reach Silas by phone, but he doesn't answer. Larkin flips on the sirens to find Silas. After a mile, Silas is nowhere to be found. They circle back and travel cross streets. Still, nothing, and now the men grow anxious by the minute.

They drive to Silas's house and see if he's there. Larkin turns off the sirens as the house comes into view. The garage door is down, but there is a vehicle in the drive. The men park at the end of the driveway, draw their weapons, and crouch low as they approach the door. They glance inside the parked vehicle and see nothing. Then, moving towards the front door, the men take up positions near the window.

Chapter 22

The door opens, and Silas steps outside, "What are you doing out here? I lost you at the traffic light. Detective Sanders is inside. Come on in."

Watson lets out an enormous sigh, and Larkin shakes his head. they enter the house and look at Detective Sanders. "You're driving your personal car, Sanders."

"Yes. I didn't want a department-issued sedan sitting out front because it would be a giveaway." He explains with a grin. "Now, do we have a photo of the guy we are looking for? Or should I suspect everyone?"

Larkin answers, "right now, all visitors are a concern. We have a description of a young guy we've been looking for, but it's not 100% complete. We have a bullet fragment we can use for comparison. The killer carries a 22-caliber handgun. Something to consider."

"Since you're situated, we'll leave you to it." Both men wave as they head out the door. On the walk down the driveway, Watson notices an older model pickup sitting in a neighbor's drive three houses down. Larkin catches Watson staring at it. "What's up, Watson?"

"I don't know. The older truck caught my eye and got me thinking. Did the crime scene tech send us the results of the tire tracks from Calon's scene?"

"Not yet. They should have something tomorrow. I'm hoping that adds to our evidence. We need more evidence to put this guy away for life." Larkin states.

With the pickup truck still on his mind, Watson climbs into the vehicle and returns to the office. He stops in the conference room after the Silas situation and asks the group for an update. Officer Rafter takes the lead. "We finished the video from the conference, and one person stands out from the rest. Titus Jett is in the crowd. Digger placed several calls to Titus with no return call. Also, Digger and Titus are meeting tomorrow at the hardware store. Zachary is meeting us here tomorrow after his shift around three."

"Interesting. Thanks for the update. Silas is at home with Detective Sanders. Now, we need to concentrate on Paul and Titus. I want to know why Titus is avoiding your calls. Can we ping his cell phone?"

"Sure, we can. Let me take a run to the investigation's division. They can ping it for us." Rafter offers.

With several things in motion, the group leans back and ponders their ideas. Paul is the most frustrating. How can someone vanish from a city street? With one piece of the picture missing, is the killer saving it for someone special, like Silas? This thought runs through everyone's mind.

Rafter trots back into the room with a grim expression. "Titus turned his phone off. So, we have no way of tracking him. He probably doesn't know Digger left messages. Also, I pinged Paul's phone and the same. It's off."

"That says something, right?" Watson states as he struggles with the reasons. "Is Paul and Titus together? Should we ask Kelly to run a story on Paul and Titus as persons of interest? Would the story help or hurt our case?"

No one opens their mouth. Unsure of the answer to Watson's questions. He looks at each person waiting for a response. When he doesn't see one coming, he sits in a chair and leans his head back while rubbing his forehead.

Larkin sits up straight before he replies, "My thoughts are to wait until tomorrow. Digger is meeting with Titus at the store, and we have Zachary's meeting at three. With these two, we'll have a clearer understanding of the situation. Although I'm 90% sure it's Titus. He fits the description, and he matches Ellie's profile. I say we put a detective on Titus when we find him. Let's see where he takes us."

All heads nod in agreement. "Do we have a young guy we can use to follow Titus? He'll catch on to an older guy following him." Ellie suggests. "He's probably feeling a little skittish, anyway. The police are gaining on him, and he's nervous."

Watson and Larkin share a look and acknowledge the suggestions. Then, Larkin faces Rafter, "Has Titus seen your smiling face yet?"

266

"No, sir," Rafter replies as he puffs out his chest. He finally gets his shot at being an undercover detective. Rafter fidgets as he waits for Larkin to continue.

"Change into plain clothes. You're going to purchase an item at the hardware store. I want to know if Titus is there."

"Yes, sir." Rafter hurries out the door for fear, Larkin might change his mind. Rafter's goal is to become a Captain of a major case squad. This is his chance. Excitement courses through his veins as he plans his strategy.

While Rafter is at the store, the group waits for his return. Digger peruses his notes again, even though he memorized most of them. He keeps thinking something is missing. The victims are all identified and associated with a halfway house. That's the connection to the killer, but what about Silas? Digger flips to Titus' sheet, and in bold letters, he sees a circle drawn around Silas's name. So, that makes sense why Titus would target Silas. But is Titus planting the notes and destroying Silas's office?

Ninety minutes pass when Rafter walks into the room. In casual clothes, it takes a few seconds for recognition to process in Digger's mind. "What's the word, Rafter? Is Titus working today?"

Rafter smiles as he produces a wrench from his back pocket. "Titus is off today from the team member schedule on the desk. He works tomorrow. His day starts at eight and ends at five tomorrow. I walked the back lot like we discussed. There are several open storage bins for landscaping material. In the back corner, there are two small metal buildings. I couldn't see the contents, and I couldn't stop and look because a team member escorted me. We discussed my landscaping options for my backyard."

Larkin's head bobs as he contemplates the layout of the lot. The hardware store is a viable location for Paul. What makes no sense is why Titus would kidnap and possibly murder Paul if his picture is complete? Did Paul take something from Titus or make fun of him? Or has Titus chosen a new image for his victims?

"We'll stop for the day. Rafter, you handle Digger's appointment with Titus tomorrow. He'll know we are on to him if he sees Digger. I'll have a detective waiting outside to follow Titus if he gets nervous. Then we wait for Zachary's visit. I think it will be a waste of time for us, but since we have it on the calendar, we should finish it."

Larkin drops everyone off at the hotel and drives to Silas's house for one more glimpse before heading home. The neighbor's truck is not in the driveway, and Larkin notices the house appears unoccupied. Newspapers litter the ground around the mailbox. Larkin pulls over to the mailbox and opens it, only to have mail fall to the ground. He crams what he can back into the box and parks his vehicle in the drive.

He stands at the lawn's edge facing Silas' house. It provides a perfect view of the front and a partial view of the backyard. Was Titus sitting in the truck when we pulled into the driveway? If so, does he think the car belongs to a friend? Larkin shakes his head, trying to clear it. He walks to the front door and knocks. When an answer doesn't come, he walks around to the back. The back of the house is in worse repair than the front.

A next-door neighbor peers over a fence, and Larkin asks, "do you know the owner of this house and how I might contact them?"

The lady shrugs and says, "I haven't seen the owners in months. They ran into money troubles and left in the night. I assume the bank owns the property now. Why are you asking?"

Larkin identifies himself by producing his badge. "There was a pickup truck parked in the driveway earlier, and I'm trying to locate it."

"The truck has been parking in the drive several times a week for a few weeks now. No one ever gets out of it. They just sit in the truck. The windows are so dark, I can't see the driver from my house. So I'm not brave enough to approach the truck."

"You shouldn't approach it. Could I give you my card, and if you see the truck again, would you call my cell phone number?" Larkin asks.

"Yes. I'll be glad too, as long as you don't tell the driver how you got the information." The lady states.

"Thank you, ma'am. You've been a big help." Larkin turns and walks back to his vehicle. He now thinks the truck belongs to Titus, and he's been watching Silas.

Larkin calls Detective Sanders and discusses the recent information. Sanders peeks out the front window, and Larkin throws up a hand. Sanders nods. With Titus' location unknown, Sanders is on alert. If an attack is imminent, he'll call 911 then Larkin. Larkin backs out of the driveway and heads home.

The following day, Bob drives the group to headquarters for the morning meeting. Larkin shares his visit with Silas's neighbor. Watson smiles because he spotted the truck in the driveway yesterday when they escorted Silas home. As the meeting continues, Rafter enters the room in casual clothes. He looks the part of a young guy learning home repair. He's set to meet Titus at ten for help with tools. Then Zachary comes in this afternoon. After these two meetings, they have no remaining leads. No other halfway house residents seem violent other than Zachary and Titus. Zachary is more apprehensive of the police than violent, where Titus is cold and calculating.

The group provides Rafter with information on Titus and questions for him to ask. They don't want to scare Titus. They are merely trying to determine where he's living since Chopper refuses to give them the information. Larkin confirms with Rafter his use of a surveillance microphone. He tapes it to his chest. Rafter leaves headquarters for his rendezvous. Detectives sit outside the store in unmarked vehicles listening to Rafter's conversations. If anything goes haywire, they'll provide backup.

While Rafter is away, Ellie reviews the notes on the skulls. Ellie frowns as she reads her letters. Both sets of skulls are identified. She can't find any remaining relatives, which is unusual. Most of her cases have at least one living relative who agrees to take responsibility for burial. Unfortunately, these two sets of skeletons seem to have no one but each other. Unshed tears sit at the brink of tumbling out of Ellie's eyes. There is nothing sadder than being alone in this world. She lifts a silent prayer of thanks for Digger. Without him in her life, she would be lonely, too, other than a handful of friends.

It's lunch, and Rafter hasn't returned to headquarters. Larkin paces in front of the windows. He gives up and calls a surveillance detective. The group gathers as Larkin listens to the detective. With little to report, the call ended quickly. Larkin looks at us and states, "Rafter is still inside with Titus. Titus was with a customer when Rafter arrived. He waited until Titus was free, causing a delay. Rafter and Titus are in the middle of the conversation. Nothing exciting yet."

Relief spreads through the group as they know Rafter is well. Their hope is for Rafter to return to headquarters with information before they meet with Zachary. Watson's phone rings and he steps off to the side to answer. The others watch his face, and they know he's speaking with Kelly. Those two seem to have formed a union. They are two different souls who like each other. One is a television reporter, and the other a special agent with the FBI. The conversation around the dinner table will be delicate at best.

A call comes through for Larkin, and Rafter is on his way back to headquarters. The group is eager to hear the outcome of Rafter's visit. Everyone sits around the table and talks while they wait. Titus is the group's choice for the killer. They must find a way to put him at the crime scene, and without physical evidence linking him, that doesn't prove easy.

Minutes later, Rafter enters the room holding the microphone in his hand. "The hardest part of the meeting is the microphone. It tickles." Laughter breaks out across the room. "Let me tell you about Titus. He is one strange fellow. His insights into world affairs are scary. Titus knows his way around a set of tools. The hardware store is lucky to have him, but the outside world, not so much. We walked to the back lot, discussing options for my backyard, and there was a strange stench emanating from the back corner toward town. Titus steered me away from the area, stating, employees only."

Larkin speaks to the group, "did you ask about his living arrangements?"

"Yes, all I got from him was he lives in an apartment complex close by the store. I wonder if he lives in the same complex as Zachary."

Watson jumps in, "I agree with Rafter. However, we need to ask Zachary this afternoon. His meeting might be useful, after all." A smile grows on Watson's face.

"We still don't have enough evidence to get a search warrant for the store. No judge will sign a warrant on a hunch. Trust me. I've tried. I'll work on the way to gain entry to the back lot." Larkin states then praise Rafter for a job well done.

Digger looks at Watson, "can you help with the warrant? We need to get this guy off the streets."

"Without evidence, my hands are tied. If we can find the gun and it matches the fragment we have, without a doubt, I can get a warrant." Watson advises.

Everyone hangs their head in frustration. Larkin paces while rubbing his neck. Then he stops and turns to the group. "What if we break into the lot at night? The owner will report the break in the following day, and we can accompany the police officers to the lot and look around."

"Not a bad idea, Larkin. The break-in will need to occur on the side where the smell is the worst. The closer to the smell, the better. We need to find out what's causing the stench. Does anyone remember if there are cameras on that side of the lot? I don't want our bad guys on camera if we can help it." Watson works the plan in his head. "Whoever breaks in will dress in all black. The only thing showing will be the eyes through their mask."

Larkin agrees with Watson's assessment. The group jots note to prepare for the next steps in the investigation. With Zachary's meeting approaching, the group slips out for lunch, except Watson. He meets Kelly for lunch.

While the group is out for lunch, Rafter checks on the status of Titus. His location has remained unknown since he left the store. He wouldn't be at Chopper's, the hardware store, or Silas's neighbor's unless he slipped in without being sighted. Digger glances at Rafter and shrugs his shoulder. Titus has murdered multiple people without being seen. He has no problem entering places unseen.

Zachary is right on time, and the group is ready to finish this meeting. The meeting starts as cordial, but then it turns confrontational. Zachary becomes agitated at the questions about the murders. He states he is not the murderer and is glad to be out on his own. Jail is not the place for him, and he'll never go back there. Zachary admits to being friends with Titus, and he confirms that he lives in the same apartment complex two doors down from him and Damon lives around the corner. He further explains Titus is strange sometimes. One day he is fine, and the next, he is quiet and withdrawn. On those days, Zachary says he leaves him alone.

The last question on Titus confirms some things for the group. Zachary advises Titus drives an older pickup truck with tinted windows. Titus told Zachary he was lucky his parents gave it to him.

Digger looks at Ellie. "Who are Titus' parents? Have we checked?"

"No, we haven't. Let's get a background check on him. He's our killer. We need to know everything we can about him." Ellie states as she presents the request to Rafter. They watch as Rafter exits the room to request the background check.

Once Zachary's meeting concludes, Digger and Ellie share their request with Larkin, and he agrees to share a photo of Titus with the SWAT members if he shows. The group acknowledges Zachary is not the killer. Everything points to Titus, just no physical evidence yet, except for the mangled bullet.

An hour later, two SWAT members enter the room dressed in black. They show Larkin the black face mask they will wear while committing the fake crime. The group discusses the area of the back fence they want the duo to cut. Once they enter, they will shift items around to make it appear someone is looking for something. The idea is to get the owner to call the police for a report of a break-in. A back-up will be close by if the need arises. The SWAT duo preps for individual video and voice communications. SWAT commander Martin refuses to let his men go ahead without their video and communications manager during the so-called crime. Commander Martin emphasizes the duo will not damage property other than the fence. The men share a glance as they exit the room.

Chapter 23

The night progresses for Larkin as he awaits word on the break-in. He can't find sleep, so he moves to his office and sits in his leather chair. Will the break-in bring the outcome they wanted? It needs to be visible enough to provoke the owner to make a report but not a lot of damage to cause the owner harm. He knows they are treading on thin ice, but he couldn't find another way to make it happen.

In the early morning hours, while the sky is still black, the break-in occurs. It takes little effort for the men to cut through the fence, leaving a gaping hole. Instead, they follow the stench and slide the door to the metal building open, exposing a body. Then, as they were instructed, they shuffled a few items and moved outdoor items around. The duo knows the exposed body will force the owner into reporting the break-in.

At 3:00 AM, Larkin receives confirmation of the break-in and body. He tries for a few hours of sleep, which is restless because he knows Paul is dead. Stirring in the bed, he rolls over to a text message. Titus had no sightings overnight, which is not a good way to start a day. You have another dead body and no killer.

Larkin checks in with the detective sitting on Silas' neighbor's house as he drives to headquarters. He has seen or heard nothing all night. The detective confirms Silas is moving around his house, probably preparing for work. When the call ends,

Larkin wants Silas to remain at home until they can locate Titus.

Calling Silas, Larkin expresses concern for his well-being. He let Silas know about Paul, and he suggested Silas work from home today. Silas refuses, stating he has court. He has to be in court for three hearings today. He has no time to sit at home. Larkin wants to reach through the phone and shake this man. Silas has no regard for his life while the rest of the police force is trying to save it.

Before meeting at the office, Ellie, Digger, and Bob visit Titus' apartment complex. With Zachary's help, they have the apartment number. They ride through the lot, looking for surveillance spots. The complex layout doesn't give many choices, and since they don't know the make of Titus' truck, they have no way of knowing if he is inside. Digger takes photos of the complex buildings with notable choices for surveillance.

On their way to headquarters, Larkin notifies Digger of the find at the hardware store. The owner just called in the body to the police, and he's following a patrol car to the store. Watson requests Digger's presence at the store. When the group arrives at the store, the police start the report at the fence. A gaping hole in the fence gives a reason for how the offenders gained access. The police officer surmises the felons ran off when they discovered the body. The owner agrees with the explanation. He also states he has never had a break-in at this location in business, nor has he had a dead body on his property.

Digger and Ellie step away from the group to discuss the body in private. "Why did the killer change his MO? A tarp covers Paul with tape across this mouth and no visible carving. He has a bullet hole in his forehead, like the others."

Ellie shakes her head as she responds, "other than being in a hurry to hide a body, I have no other explanation. I would like to see the body when the medical examiner unwraps it. The killer might have another message tied up in the tarp."

Digger stares at Ellie as he processes her words, "another message? What do you mean?"

"The killer left a message in the form of the carvings on every other victim so far. So why would Paul be left out?" Ellie looks at Digger while he works through the statements.

More people enter the back lot. Ellie and Digger crane their heads so they can see who is joining the scene. "It's the medical examiner. Let's follow him and see what happens when they remove Paul."

The medical examiner takes over the scene while they process the body. The police stand around waiting for the body's removal. As soon as the medical examiner opens the bag, Larkin confirms the identity. It's Paul. There is a note taped to his shirt. It states, "you are missing one."

Everyone looks around the group. Ellie and Digger cringe. "You were right, Ellie. He left a message."

"Great. Being right isn't always fun. Has anyone checked on the public defenders this morning? Also, Larkin now might be a good time to discuss Titus with the owner."

Larkin advises he spoke with Silas this morning, and all three have court today with multiple cases on the docket. He also had a brief conversation with the store owner about Titus. Today is Titus's scheduled off day. With this information, Larkin issues a BOLO for Titus.

A massive city-wide search starts for Titus. The police patrol all known places, and he's nowhere to be found. Police officers sit at Chopper's, which makes him mad. He repeats how the police upset his residents. Digger explains the consequences, and Chopper settles. Chopper calls Titus so he can talk him into turning himself into the police. Titus's phone is off.

Later in the afternoon, the group stops by to visit Silas at the courthouse. As they pass the lot, Watson points out the entrance to Bob. Then, Bob points to a young guy standing next to a car. "Hey, is that Titus? Who is that standing with him?"

All heads swivel, turning to find the guy. Watson says, "we have a problem. Titus is holding Silas by the neck, and someone is talking to them. Park across the street. We're going in on foot."

Bob finds a spot and pulls in. Watson, Bob, and Larkin pull their weapons and creep toward Silas. They hear Detective Sanders speaking with Titus, but Titus doesn't care. He knows his murder spree is over, and he's ready for it to end.

Larkin's intrusion catches Titus off guard, and he fires his gun at Larkin. Larkin ducks behind a vehicle. During the melee, the bullet crazes Silas's upper arm. He lets out a growl and reaches for his arm. Blood seeps between his fingers and runs down his arm.

After the fired shot, Titus turns his attention to Silas. Unfortunately, he doesn't see Larkin and Watson approach from the side and the rear. When Titus looks up and realizes no one faces him, he spins around, still holding Silas. As he does, Larkin tackles Titus from behind, and Watson cuffs him. EMS arrives within minutes to treat and transport Silas to the emergency room.

Titus sits alone in an interview room at police headquarters. Watson takes the lead with Ellie and Digger by his side. Ellie speaks with Titus in a calm, quiet manner. Then he gives up his last kill by stating the victim lives in an RV parked in an out-of-the-way location. Watson speaks with Larkin about the recent murder so he can dispatch police to the location. Titus changes topics as he offers his thanks for showing his grandparents on the television.

Digger's head snaps up, and he says, "your grandparents?" Digger pulls photos of the skulls out of a folder and lays them face up on the table. "This set is your parents, The Teeter's, and this set is your grandparents, The Anderson's."

"Yep. My mom had me before she became a Teeter. No way was I going through school with the last Teeter. I kept my dad's name- Jett." Titus explains and smiles.

It surprises Digger in one way but not others that Titus murdered his family. But Titus's mind is twisted in a way no one can understand but him. While Digger finishes with Titus, Larkin receives confirmation of the last murder victim. Titus locked the victim in an RV without air conditioning for weeks, leaving the body in terrible shape. The medical examiner is en route for body recovery.

Titus sits behind bars as the FBI ponders the death sentence. The killer hasn't shown remorse, just fascination with the people that tracked him. He never explained why he killed his family, and for the authorities, it doesn't matter. To know they located and identified all the murdered bodies is enough for them.

The team spends their last night together putting the final touches on the Titus Jett killing spree. After a visit with Silas at the hospital, Digger and Ellie hit the road for home.

Other Books by A.M. Holloway

Series Books

Flames of Murder (Mac Morris Thriller Book 2)

Promises of Murder (Sheriff Jada Steele Book 1)

Pieces of Murder (Digger Collins Thriller Book 1)

MOA (Mac Morris Thriller Book 1)

~~~~~~

Visit www.amholloway.com to sign up for

my reader's list and updates

or simply scan the code.

Made in the USA
Las Vegas, NV
14 October 2022

57268737R00164